W9-BJU-394

# *Marathon Miranda*

ELIZABETH WINTHROP

# *Marathon Miranda*

**HOLIDAY HOUSE**
**New York**

*Library of Congress Cataloging in Publication Data*

Winthrop, Elizabeth.
  Marathon Miranda.

  SUMMARY: Miranda feels left out of everything until
she meets a jogger in training for a marathon. Despite
her apprehension about a sudden attack of asthma,
Miranda starts to run.
  [1. Running—Fiction. 2. Adoption—Fiction]
I. Title.
PZ7.W768Mar    [Fic]    78-20615
ISBN 0-8234-0349-1

*For my cousin Anne*
*who taught me everything*

# Contents

# Marathon Miranda

# 1 • I Get Asthma

I hate baseball. The game takes too long, especially when the kids in my school play, because usually the pitcher can't pitch and the batter can't bat. But the real trouble is I'm allergic to it. Not to baseball but to the field. All that grass and dust and pollen. I just look down, and I start to wheeze.

The funny thing about this time was I didn't wheeze in the beginning. I was fine when I stepped up to bat. Then I hit this stupid short shot and started to run. By the time I got to first base I was a goner. Viola was playing first base. She looked at me standing there with my collarbone sticking way out and that rasping sound coming from my chest, and she turned away. Viola has never forgiven me for winning the English prize last year. She was sure she was going to get it. I heard her telling her friend Debbie that I was a faker, and I just had asthma to get attention.

So right in the middle of the next batter's hit I had to limp back to home plate.

"Hey, Miranda, you're going the wrong way," Ellen shouted as she ran past.

I just pointed to my chest and waved her by.

Mr. Jackson, the gym teacher, has gotten used to my asthma, but even he looked scared when he heard this attack. The problem is we play baseball in Central Park, and he has to decide whether to bring the whole class in or send me back to school with a friend.

He sat me down on a bench and brought me my inhaler. Awful stuff. It makes me gag but it does clear out my chest a bit.

The game had stopped and everybody was hanging around watching me. I'm sure they thought I was faking.

"Mr. Jackson, it's better now. I'll just go back to school and see the nurse." I took a deep breath and it sounded awful. My chest was really hurting. "Please start the game up again," I whispered.

"Okay, next batter up," he shouted.

My friend Katherine came trotting over and grinned at me. "Usual routine?" she asked. She keeps telling me she hates baseball too so it doesn't bother

her to have to walk me back to school.

"It's a little worse than usual," I gasped. "Can't figure out why." I took another deep breath but it didn't help. When you're having an asthma attack you try breathing with little short breaths because they don't hurt as much. Then every so often, you take one big breath which gives you an awful pain in the chest and clears things out all at the same time.

I didn't feel like moving but I wasn't going to sit there and watch everybody watching me. I could see dumb old Viola snickering with her friends.

"Let's move out," I said.

"Are you sure you're ready?" Katherine asked.

I nodded. I took another shot of the medicine, and we started off. It was a long walk back to school.

"Go slower," Katherine kept saying. "Then I don't have to come back again." She was kidding me to cover up how nervous she felt. I was making a lot of noise, and people kept stopping to stare at me.

The nurse gave me one of my pills. "This is the third attack this week, Miranda. I think you should be excused from baseball. Have your mother call the doctor about it."

The last time we went to see the doctor, he gave me this big lecture about starting to build up my lung capacity and the need for physical exercise. It seemed the wrong time to ask him for a gym excuse.

I was still feeling pretty awful after sitting in the

nurse's office for an hour, so she called a cab and sent me home. Both my parents work, so I went to Margaret's apartment.

She didn't look surprised to see me.

"The baseball again?" she asked with a little smile. I nodded. "Are you busy?"

"No. You're just in time for tea. Sit over there on the couch. Have you taken the medicine?"

"Yes. It's taking a long time to work though."

"Just sit there and relax while I get the tea. I've got some chocolate cake here, too."

Margaret lives on the third floor of our building. When we first moved in, she brought my parents a bottle of wine and a cake. She's that kind of person. Never bugs you, but she's always there when you need her. She used to stay with Alex, my older brother, when I had an attack and my parents had to take me to the hospital in the middle of the night.

Ever since I was about seven years old, Margaret and I have gone on trips. She really knows the special places in the city.

"You'd better be all right by tomorrow," Margaret said. She handed me a cup of tea with honey and a huge piece of chocolate cake.

"Don't worry. I'm coming even if I have to wheeze all the way there." The next day we were going on our annual spring trip to the Bronx Zoo. Every year we go to a different place in the zoo.

"Have you been to the World of Birds?" she asked.

I shook my head. My mouth was too full of cake to say anything.

"You'll like it, Miranda. There's one room where the birds fly around your head, and at two o'clock there is a tropical rainstorm. I was there the week it opened."

Margaret belongs to every museum, zoo, and theater in New York City. That's what I love about her. She's still full of life even though she must be sixty-five or seventy. She's not like those crabby old people who sit on the benches in Riverside Park and complain about the garbage in the streets and the crime rates.

"Did you hear about Mr. Kent up in 12E?"

Margaret shook her head. This time her mouth was full of cake. She likes sweets just as much as I do. We both drive my brother Alex crazy. Besides being an amateur psychiatrist and a weight lifter, he's also a health food nut.

"He had a fire in his wastepaper basket last night and when he couldn't put it out with a glass of water, he opened the window and threw the whole thing out. Can you imagine? Twelve floors. It sounded like a stick of dynamite when it hit the pavement."

"He was lucky it didn't hit anybody," Margaret said. "That man is insane."

Margaret and I have been keeping an eye on Mr.

Kent ever since he kicked my dog, Frisbee, one morning just because she was sniffing his shoe.

Once you've lived in an apartment building long enough, you get hooked on it. It's like belonging to one big family except everybody has his own privacy. My grandfather lives on a farm in Vermont and refuses to come to New York because he hates the feeling of people squished up next to him. Like a lot of pigs, he once said. But my mother could never move to the country. She says she would feel too lonely.

"More cake, Miranda?"

I secretly wanted more but I was too embarrassed to admit it.

"It seems to have cured the asthma," Margaret said with a smile.

I'd almost stopped wheezing. "I'd better not. Thanks. It was delicious."

"The bakery's best. I'll wrap up a piece for your dessert tonight. Just be sure Alex doesn't see it. I was subjected to one of his nutrition tirades in the elevator the other day. It took me a trip to Baskin-Robbins for a double peppermint stick cone to recover."

Margaret burst out laughing at her own joke. She has a wonderful laugh. Very deep and hearty, like a man's.

"Do you want to help me do the plants?" she asked.

"All right." Margaret is a plant freak. She must have at least two hundred plants in her apartment. She's been trying to get me interested in them but I can't seem to catch on. Last weekend, she went away and when I watered her plants, I accidentally dropped water on the leaves of her favorite glox-something or other. The leaves all died.

"You do the ones in the bedroom," Margaret said, handing me the smaller watering can. "Remember to check the soil first. Don't just drown them."

Her two black cats were asleep on the bed, curled into semicircles. I stopped and looked at the photographs on the bureau. There was an old brown one of a very handsome man with a mustache and a bowler hat. That was Margaret's husband. He worked in the garment district in New York. They used to own a brownstone in Brooklyn, and he died of a heart attack very suddenly when he was only fifty-five. That was when Margaret moved into this apartment and went to work for a travel magazine. They sent her on trips all around the world. The walls of her bedroom are covered with elephants' tusks and African masks and a mummy's hand in a glass case and an old Japanese scroll.

"Miranda, are you finished? It's almost five o'clock, and I've got to do an errand on Broadway."

"Coming," I said, splashing some water over the last few plants.

"Don't forget your cake," she said as I headed for the door.

"Thanks, Margaret. See you tomorrow."

"Meet me in the lobby around nine o'clock. We want to be there when the zoo opens, and the subways are slow on Saturday."

My mother was home from work when I got in.

"I was beginning to worry about you," she said. "Frisbee is going to drive us mad if you don't take her out soon. Where have you been?"

"Down at Margaret's. I had to come home from school early."

"Baseball again? Another asthma attack?"

"Yes. It was worse than usual. I hate it. All the kids stared at me, and I know Viola Dawson is telling everybody that I'm faking it."

"Imagine calling your child Viola," my mother said.

"Miranda isn't exactly your everyday name either, Mother."

"But it's prettier, don't you think?" she asked.

I didn't answer. I like my mother but sometimes she drives me crazy because she's a terrible romantic. Plus the fact she goes off the track when I'm trying to have a serious conversation. But this time she got back on it.

"Well, if you're not faking the asthma, what do you care what the other kids say?"

"I'll take Frisbee out," I said. There are some questions I don't know how to answer.

My mother didn't seem to notice. She was standing in front of the refrigerator, trying to think of something. She is the personnel director for the Sheraton Hotel, and she often comes home from work in a daze. The things she runs into at that job would put anybody in a daze, not to mention an insane asylum. My father keeps telling her to write a book, but she says she doesn't have the energy to do anything creative at the end of the day. "How about being a mother?" my brother always says. "Doesn't that take creative energy?" My brother likes to sit around analyzing the rest of us.

"Is Alex home?"

My mother nodded. "Oh, there they are." She plunged into the refrigerator and came out with a package of pork chops. "I was sure I had forgotten to defrost them."

"I think Pops took them out after you left," I said.

"See, I was right. I had forgotten to defrost them," she said triumphantly.

I shook my head and went out the front door, whistling for Frisbee.

# 2 · The World of Birds

"Your mother says you had asthma again at baseball today," Pops said to me at dinner. The asthma comes down through his side of the family so he feels kind of guilty about it.

"Yes." I shrugged. "It got me out of baseball."

"Asthma is supposed to be a psychosomatic disease," Alex said in his lecturing voice. "Miranda doesn't like baseball, therefore Miranda gets asthma."

"I don't think it's that simple, Alex," my father said.

I didn't say anything. Whenever I try to defend myself against Alex, I sound guilty.

"Well, you don't have to sleep in the same room with her, Pops. When she starts that wheezing at night, it sounds like a storm out of the northwest."

I smiled in spite of myself. Some of the things Alex says are pretty funny.

"I've been thinking about that. You two are getting too old to share a room, and you know we can't afford a bigger apartment because of the school bills. So I was thinking we could put up a partition in your room to divide it. There are two windows so both of you'd have some light."

Alex and I looked at each other. We each knew what the other was thinking.

"Which one of us would get the view?" I asked.

"That's something you would have to work out between you," my father said.

"Why don't you talk it over and let us know what you decide," said Mother. "We don't have to do it right away."

I loved the idea of my own room. The only time I have privacy is when we go for our annual August visit to my grandfather's house in Vermont. Nothing's sacred when you've got a fourteen-year-old brother living in the top bunk. Especially when he's a brother who's decided to be a psychiatrist.

I know we don't have the money to move. My father is a free-lance artist and with the rent on his studio and our school bills, we are stretched very thin. But our apartment is in a building on Riverside Drive, and we have a fantastic view of the Hudson River. I'm not sure I'd like to give that up just to have a wall between me and Alex.

"I made the dessert," Alex said, carrying in this huge bowl of glop.

"Oh, no," I groaned. "It will look beautiful and taste awful." Sometimes Alex gets it in his head to start cooking. The trouble is he gets all wrapped up in the way the food looks. He usually forgets some basic ingredient.

"Tapioca pudding à la mint," he announced, setting the dish down in front of us. We studied it carefully. There were a lot of mint leaves stuck around the edge of the pudding and one fat strawberry in the middle.

"It looks terrific, Alex," my mother said.

"Dish it up," Pops said.

"Not too much for me," I said quickly. Alex gave me a dark look. "I'm on a diet," I added with a sweet smile.

"Oh, no, Miranda," my mother cried. I weigh about twenty-two pounds and look like some kind of orphan with my skinny arms and legs.

"Mother, that's a joke. She's just afraid I'm going to poison her," said Alex. He heaped two huge spoonfuls of glop on my plate.

We each took a bite.

"What an interesting taste, Alex," Mother said. She likes to encourage my brother in his cooking efforts. That's because I haven't shown much interest at all.

"You left out the sugar," I said, putting down my spoon.

"Yes, that's it," said Pops. "I couldn't quite decide what was wrong."

"A master chef should not be bothered with such details," Alex announced, waving his spoon in the air grandly. A clump of tapioca sailed off and hit the window. Mother wiped it off with her napkin.

"Easy does it," she said dryly.

"River alert," I said. A huge tanker was coming down the river. At night, they run up and back to Albany with just three or four lights on. They are like huge silent fish drifting with the current.

"Can you see which one it is?" Pops asked.

"Too dark," said Mother.

We keep a river diary up on the kitchen wall. Anybody who sees a boat writes down the name and the time and the direction it's going. That way we keep track of the traffic on the river. The only trouble is that none of us is there during the day.

That night when we were going to bed, Alex asked me what I thought of Pops' idea.

"It would be nice to get away from you," I said slowly, "but I wouldn't want to give up the view." The view from our window is the best in the apartment. It looks north to the George Washington Bridge.

"That's the way I feel," Alex said. "I'd rather keep things the way they are."

"I'm sure you would. If I moved into my own room, you would lose your most interesting case, Dr. Bartlett," I said.

"Oh, dry up, Sis."

I can't stand it when he calls me Sis.

"Everybody in school thinks it's really weird that I still sleep in the same room with my brother," I said.

Alex snorted. "Why? Do they think I'm going to rape you or something?"

"Come on, Alex, don't be gross," I muttered. Even though I knew he was joking, we really were getting too old to share the same room.

I was the first one down in the lobby the next morning. Margaret is always late for everything. She tries to pack too much into a day.

"Sorry, Miranda," she said, barreling out of the elevator. "I just had this one letter to finish."

I smiled. Margaret looked as if she were going on an African safari. She had on one of those canvas jungle hats with the wide brim, khaki pants, and her brown walking shoes. There was a pair of binoculars slung one way across her chest and a camera slung the other.

"Dr. Livingston, I presume?" I said in a deep voice.

"I believe in traveling well equipped," she said haughtily.

The elevator door opened again and Mother walked out.

"Haven't you two left yet?" she asked.

"It's my fault," Margaret said.

We all walked out the front door together. Richard, the doorman, patted my shoulder. "Good morning, Miranda. Off on a trip?" I didn't answer. Richard's been around the building since we moved in. He keeps reminding me that he used to see me pushed to the playground in my carriage. Drives me up the wall.

Mother decided to take the crosstown bus with us. She was going shopping.

As soon as we got on the bus, I knew we were in for it. There was a crazy lady sitting in the back talking to herself. My mother has this theory that those people need someone to listen to their troubles. So whenever she sees someone like that, she goes and sits next to them. Of course, she's probably right because nobody else in the bus ever gets near them.

"Let's sit here, Mother," I said, plumping myself down near the door. But she was already headed for the back.

Margaret sat next to me. "There she goes again," I said, pointing to Mother. The crazy lady had started up a conversation.

"Your mother is too kind for her own good," Margaret said.

"Sometimes when I think of her going through a day in New York, I almost want to cry," I said. "It's like letting a kid out in the street when he's still too young. The other day she said excuse me to this rude fat lady who pushed in front of her at the fruit stand."

Margaret smiled. "She's a good listener. That's why she does so well at that job."

Margaret's right. For all her absentmindedness my mother is a very good listener.

When the bus crossed Park Avenue, I glanced toward the back. The lady was holding Mother's arm and waving her finger under her nose.

"Looks like she needs to be rescued again," I said, getting up. "Mother, we get off at the next stop."

"I'm coming, Miranda." She tried to stand up but the lady kept holding on and talking loudly. I was about to die. Everyone in the bus was watching.

Margaret brushed past. She swooped down on the pair of them, removed the crazy lady's hand, and led Mother out of the bus like a little girl. We could still hear the woman shouting as the bus started up again. Thank heavens for Margaret. She can take care of anything.

"That poor woman," Mother said. "She was talking about some terrible man who had taken away all her furniture."

"If Margaret hadn't rescued you, you'd still be there this afternoon," I said. "Now, Mother, do you think you can get downtown without us?"

"I do it every day by myself, Miranda," she said giving me a kiss on the cheek. "Have a good day," she called as she went down the subway steps.

Even though we were later than we meant to be, the zoo wasn't crowded when we arrived. Margaret marched me past the giraffes and elephants and the World of Darkness, my favorite place of all. She's always firm about doing what we came for first when we go on our trips. "That's the only way you really learn something," she once told me.

This bird house is amazing. It's built like a lot of doughnuts sitting on top of each other with ramps coming out at different levels. When you go in, you start at the bottom and look at the birds that live near the ground. By the time you're finished, you're looking at the birds who live in the treetops. Halfway through there's this wonderful tropical room where the most amazing birds fly around right above your head. Margaret and I spent the most time there. She is very good at standing still and waiting till the birds settle down. She's always seeing things that I'd completely miss. "That comes from a lifetime of looking," she said to me once. "I've had more practice than you."

"Now, Miranda, do you see that clump of red flowers straight ahead of you? Look a little to the right on that single branch sticking out. See him?"

I nodded. "What a funny-looking bird. What is he?"

"The Australian kookaburra. A large kingfisher. Makes a sound just like his name. Now move the binoculars up a little and to the left. See the one with the yellow crest? That's a cockatoo. His mate is sitting in the bush just below him. She's much duller looking."

"I think it's unfair the female birds are always some boring brown color," I said as we walked out.

"It does make me wonder what the good Lord was thinking about when he created the birds and the beasts," Margaret answered.

But I wasn't listening. Standing there at one of the windows was creepy old Viola Dawson with my friend Katherine. I couldn't believe my eyes. I was sure Katherine couldn't stand Viola. What was she doing going to the Bronx Zoo with her?

"Look up here, Miranda," Margaret said. "There's a—"

"I'm going on to the next room, Margaret. There's something I want to see there." I rushed out before she could answer.

When Margaret caught up with me I was standing in front of a noisy macaw who kept tapping on the glass with his beak.

"He can't get out, can he?" I asked.

"I hope not. He looks fierce. Why did you rush away? There were some wonderful lizards crawling up the trees in that room."

"There were some kids from school I didn't want to see," I said with a shrug.

"I thought it had to be something. Let's have lunch before they catch up with us," Margaret said, ushering me out. She knows how funny I am about seeing people I know. We were in Woolworth's once, buying a birthday present for my father, and I spent most of the time sneaking around the aisles avoiding a math teacher I had in school the year before. I'm always sure people aren't going to recognize me or something, so it's easier not to say hello. It saves everybody a lot of embarrassment. Now if Alex heard that, he'd really go to town. He's always telling me I don't make friends easily because I'm scared of taking chances. That's a lot of hogwash. I'm just a loner by nature.

Over lunch, I asked Margaret about her love life. That's an old joke between us. Margaret goes out with these grandfatherly-looking gentlemen who take her to the theater and the movies. I'm sure they've all asked her to marry them a hundred times but Margaret says it's not true, and I'm just being a romantic.

"Well, I do have a new man in my life," she said with a little smile. "Very shocking since he's a lot younger. My friends say he's after my money." She burst out laughing. "Too bad I don't have much."

"What's his name?"

"Steven Delaney. Doesn't that sound romantic? Actually, he's an actor on television. Advertisements and soap operas. He's waiting for that big break on Broadway. He's thin and tall, and he has dark brown hair that's going a bit gray around the ears. You'll have to meet him, Miranda. He's very special," she added in a low voice.

Well, this was something. She had never said that about any of the others. I didn't much like the sound of him, but then I'm particular about anyone who gets to be with Margaret. She's really my best friend. Especially now that Katherine's hanging around with nerdy old Viola.

## 3 · I Meet Phoebe

When I woke up the next morning, Alex was down on the floor doing his exercises. He is a maniac about physical fitness. He and his friend Peter lift weights. Isn't that ridiculous? A fourteen-year-old lifting weights. Peter lives nearby. He keeps the weights over at his place. Thank heavens. I really would move out if I had to trip over a bunch of barbells every day.

I lifted my head slowly, looked at Alex, and collapsed back on my pillow with a groan.

"Rise and shine. We cook breakfast this morning, remember?" Alex said.

We cook for my parents every Sunday morning. We figure it's the least they deserve after working all week. The only trouble is the food doesn't taste too good. Alex spends so much time making everything look right that by the time he carries the tray into their bedroom, the eggs are usually stuck to the plate. Mother and Pops are pretty brave about the whole thing, although lately Mother has been suggesting we eat out on Sunday mornings.

"Well, maestro, what is the delicacy this morning?" I asked as I pulled on my jeans. "Kippered herring with smoked salmon on the side? Shirred eggs in Hollandaise sauce? Baked Alaska?"

Alex fixed me with his beady eyes. "I've already been to the deli, slug-a-bed. As a matter of fact, it's bagels, cream cheese, and lox, with poached eggs for dessert."

"Blech." The trouble with this plan is that I'm not a breakfast person. By the time we get through, I'm ready to go back to bed. Or at least my stomach is.

"Listen, you ungrateful wretch, I took Frisbee with me to the store, so now you don't have to walk her."

"That was nice of you, Alex. Thanks." Sometimes my brother surprises me. Also I've discovered I can shut him up by saying something nice to him. He doesn't know how to handle that.

The only thing to cook was the poached eggs, but luckily we have this special pan. I timed the eggs to come out just as Alex finished the trays, so the whole process was quite painless. His final touch was a piece of our bay tree stuck into a bud vase.

"I don't think Mother's going to like that too much," I said as we walked down the hall.

"She won't recognize it," Alex said. "Pops is the one who waters all the plants."

"Breakfast is served," Alex proclaimed loudly as we burst into the room. I saw the hesitation on Mother's face as she looked over the trays. She seemed relieved when she saw what was there.

"This looks delicious," she said. And I think she meant it.

"The Atlantic Cement barge is headed down-river," Pops said.

"I'll mark it down," I said. "I have to go fix the coffee."

Atlantic Cement had gone up Saturday morning. Quick turnaround for them. When people ask me how I can bear living in New York City, I explain that we live right on the Hudson River. As far as I'm concerned there's nowhere else in the world to be. The city right at your back door but you don't have to look at it.

Later that morning, I took Frisbee for a long walk in Riverside Park. It was a beautiful day. Early spring so the first buds and the daffodils were just out. I thought of going over to Central Park but decided against it. Central Park on a nice Sunday is mobbed, and I didn't think I could face the crowds and the steel-drum bands and the hot-dogging skateboarders and the earnest joggers. Somedays that scene is what I want, but this particular Sunday I felt like some peace and quiet. Which is just what I would have gotten if that girl hadn't started talking to me.

Frisbee started the whole thing. She made friends with her dog. That's not like Frisbee at all. We usually walk along together in a leisurely way. But I can see what got to her. This dog was a golden retriever too, and they looked absolutely alike. Right down to their size and the expression on their faces.

When I looked around to see who the other dog belonged to, I saw a girl jogging along in a blue running suit with a green stripe. Blech. All this running business drives me up the wall. People in New York are such exercise freaks. Now that everybody has discovered that running along a sidewalk for twenty minutes is considered good exercise, the entire population of the Upper West Side spends twenty minutes a day running along a sidewalk. But of course you can't just run in your old sneakers and your cut-off blue jeans. Oh no. You have to buy special bright-blue sneakers and forty-dollar running outfits. It positively ruins my view in the morning to look out the window and see people doing pushups and sit-ups on the park benches and waving their arms in the air like a lot of silly windmills. Lucky thing I can't run two feet without starting to wheeze. Otherwise I might get sucked into the whole mess.

"They must be brother and sister," this girl said to me. "I've never seen two dogs look so much alike."

Well, I was thinking exactly the same thing but I didn't want to say so. That's the kind of dumb conversation dog owners have with each other at six-thirty in the morning when they're out walking their dogs. Those clusters of people standing around talking while their dogs sniff each other. They look like a bunch of mothers in the playground hovering over their children.

I just nodded at this girl and kept on walking. I wasn't going to get into any dog conversation.

"Actually, Dungeon isn't my dog. He belongs to the people across the hall. They pay me five dollars a week to walk him every day."

"I think people shouldn't have dogs in the city unless they walk them. A retriever needs a lot of exercise."

She shrugged. "I give him the exercise. Anyway, my parents won't let me have a dog, so I just pretend Dungeon belongs to me." By this time she had slowed down to my pace. "I'm running almost two miles a day, so Dungeon gets lots of exercise."

I kind of liked this girl. She had a nice friendly face, and she looked about my age.

"Dungeon is a strange name for a golden retriever. Seems to me it would sound better on a black lab."

The girl smiled. "I never thought of that. Isn't that dumb of me?"

I whistled at Frisbee, who was running up a hill toward the street. She turned around and looked at me. Then she slowly padded back toward us.

"What's her name?"

"Frisbee."

"That's great."

There was a silence. Well, now she'll just jog on, I thought to myself. No reason to creep along at my pace.

"You'd better keep running. You might lose your momentum or something," I said.

"That's all right. I already did two miles this morning."

"You run twice a day?" I asked.

"Sometimes," she said, looking out at the river. "Depends on whether I feel like getting out of the house or not . . ." Her voice drifted off.

"Do you run?" she asked after a while.

"No. I think the whole thing is a little ridiculous. A decent person can't take a simple walk without getting knocked down by some red-faced huffer and puffer. Just the other day, I went to sit on a park bench and some lady was doing her sit-ups right there. I couldn't believe it."

"Oh, come on, you're kidding."

I grinned. "To tell the truth, I wasn't going to sit there. I saw her from our bathroom window when I was brushing my teeth. But look at all these people with their matching suits and their silly-looking shoes." I had certainly picked the right moment to make my point. The promenade was full of runners as far as the eye could see. "Every type here today," I said. "Shufflers, sweaters, waddlers, high-steppers, fast walkers, and the good old huffers and puffers."

The girl burst out laughing, which was pretty nice since I suddenly remembered she had on a matching suit and silly-looking shoes. Besides, I like someone who can laugh at herself.

"Well, what kind of exercise do you do?" she asked.

"As little as possible." I shrugged. "I have asthma so I'm not supposed to exercise."

"Oh," she said in an apologetic voice. People usually act that way when they hear about my asthma.

"Have you ever tried running?" she asked. "Maybe it would build up your lungs."

"Listen, I can't even make it to first base in baseball practice. Two miles. It sounds to me like you're ready for the Olympics."

"I'm training. I want to go into a marathon this fall. Six point two miles in Central Park."

"Well, good luck," I said. We had reached 72nd

Street. I was trying to decide whether to turn around and head north or make some excuse about an errand I had to do.

"My name's Phoebe Livingston," she said suddenly. "My family just moved here from the East Side. We live in 155 Riverside. The corner of Eighty-eighth. Where do you live?"

"One sixty. Across the street from you."

"Really?" she asked. "That's great. I don't know anybody over here because I go to school on the East Side. What's your name?"

"Miranda Bartlett," I mumbled.

"Well, that's two of us," she said.

"What do you mean?"

"Miranda and Phoebe. What a pair of names."

I looked at her, and we both laughed. "Better than Jennifer," I said. "There are three Jennifers in my class."

There was a silence. I called to Frisbee.

"I have to go up to Broadway," she said quickly. "An errand for my mother. Maybe I'll see you in the park again."

"Probably," I mumbled, moving off. "See you around."

On the way home, I turned to Frisbee. "Well, what did you think of Dungeon? The lean, lanky type. He ought to be if he runs two miles a day." Frisbee turned up her nose and went off to investigate a flock of pigeons.

Nice girl, I thought to myself. I wonder if she really had an errand to do for her mother.

# 4 • Margaret's Younger Man

It's strange how you can live in the same neighbor-
hood with someone and never notice them. Then
one day you meet them and suddenly there they are
every time you turn around. Phoebe and I seemed to
have the same schedule. Two days later I saw her on
the crosstown bus. We were both going to school. I
noticed her first, and I hid behind my book. I was
sure she wouldn't remember me.

"Hi," she said, plunking herself down beside me.
"Remember me?"

I looked up slowly as if I were completely en-
grossed in my reading.

"Oh, hi," I said.

We were both silent.

"Are you going to school?" she asked.

"Yes."

"Me too." Then she got out some big book and started to read. I glanced over at the title.

"I've got that book in history too," I said. "Where are you?"

"The Middle Ages," she said, rolling her eyes. "Boring. I always do my history in the bus. I hate it."

"Oh," I said and went back to my book.

We both got off at the same bus stop on Madison.

"Where do you go to school?" she asked.

"Country Day. Up on Ninety-first Street."

"I'm at Sacred Heart. It's just the next block." We both turned to go. "Maybe I'll see you here again."

"Okay. Bye."

Then sure enough, I saw her the next afternoon running with Dungeon. I was walking up the hill above her, so she didn't see me. I stopped and watched her for a while.

"She does look pretty good in the striped suit," I said to Frisbee as we turned away. "Better than a lot of these other idiots."

Frisbee trotted ahead without looking at me.

"A girl came by and asked for you," the doorman said when I walked in. "She had a dog that looked just like yours." Richard and Frisbee don't like each other too much.

"Oh, thanks."

"I rang up to your apartment, but your brother

said you were out. She had on one of those fancy running suits."

"Thanks, Richard."

Richard was probably dying to know who Phoebe was and where she lived, but I sure wasn't going to tell him.

"Someone came to see you," Alex said when I came in.

"I know. Richard told me. It must have been that girl I met in the park on Sunday. She sure is friendly."

"Maybe's she's just charmed by your irresistible personality," Alex said with a grin.

"Maybe," I said vaguely.

The following Monday I met Margaret's young man. I was walking Frisbee down the promenade. Someone called me, and when I looked up, I saw Margaret sitting on a park bench with this man. They were holding hands. I almost dropped dead. She waved, and I walked over slowly.

"Hello, Miranda," she said cheerily. Just her old self as if nothing were different. "This is my friend Steven Delaney. I think I've mentioned him to you."

"Hello," I said in a sort of dull voice.

"Nice to meet you, Miranda," he said. He smoothed back his hair with his free hand.

"Miranda and I are very good friends. We do a lot of city exploring together. Just last week we went to the World of Birds, that new building that's opened at the Bronx Zoo. Have you been there, Steven? It's fascinating." Well, Margaret went right on chatting about this and that, and I nodded my head and pretended to pay attention, but all the time I was checking him out. He was wearing loafers, the expensive ones with the little buckles. A pair of very smooth khakis, the kind that always look pressed. A shirt and a V-necked sweater. All very fancy. He was rubbing Frisbee behind the ears. He obviously liked dogs. And I didn't like him, but I wasn't sure why.

"Have you walked north up the path by the river? Steven and I were just there. The cherry trees will be blooming any day now."

"No. Not yet. Do you live over here?" I asked Steven.

"No. East Seventy-second Street. It's a new world over here. Margaret's very proud of the West Side." He turned and gave her a smile, which very definitely left me out.

"My dog needs a run," I said, looking at Frisbee, who was sitting very still under his hand. Traitor. "See you later," I said, moving off. Frisbee finally came after the third whistle.

"Creep," I said, but I wasn't sure whether I meant Frisbee or that man.

I was walking back up the hill when somebody else

called my name. This was getting strange. It turned out to be Phoebe.

I stopped and she caught up with me.

"I've been calling you for almost a whole block." She was gasping.

"Sorry. Guess I was thinking pretty hard."

She fell into step with me. Dungeon came up behind and nudged Frisbee.

"I ran terribly today," she said. "I could barely go a mile. Must be the weather or something."

"Maybe you're running too much."

She shook her head. "I don't just do it for the exercise, though. It gives me some time to think."

"I know what you mean. I do a lot of thinking when I'm walking Frisbee."

She smiled at me suddenly as if she were happy that we had some things in common.

"Listen, do you think I could come up to your place for a while?" she asked. "My mother's in a bad mood today, and I don't want to face her yet."

"Sure," I said. I was a little surprised. I would never have the nerve to invite myself up to somebody's apartment.

I was praying that Alex wouldn't be home, but of course there he was, lying on the floor with his feet up in the air. Every week he's on some new crazy exercise program. This one has something to do with circulation. I gave him a look as if to say, my territory this afternoon, but he didn't budge.

"Phoebe, this is my brother, Alex, world-famous psychoanalyst and body builder."

"Miranda, some day you are going to regret all the terrible things you say about me." Finally, he put his feet down and sat up so he looked halfway normal. "Hello, Phoebe."

"Phoebe is a jogger. You two should get along very well," I said, sitting down on the bed.

"Do you run every day?" Alex asked.

"Just about. It's great. Unwinds the mind."

"I'm thinking about taking up the sport," Alex said.

"Alex, if you do any more exercise, your body is going to turn into one great big, disgusting muscle."

"I'm just trying to make up for you, Miranda. Well, I'll leave you two in peace." And he went out of the room. Thank heavens.

"Brothers," I said with a roll of the eyeballs.

"I think you're lucky to have one. I'm an only child and that can be a drag." She went over to the window. "My parents are big worry warts. You have a fabulous view."

"Don't you have a view of the river? From the way our doorman talks, your building has the biggest apartments on the West Side."

"Well, our apartment is probably bigger than this one, but most of the windows look east. When you

look north up the park like this, you could almost be
a million miles away from the city."

"That's why I love it. But it means I have to share
the bedroom with Alex. My parents offered to divide
the room up. I guess we'll do it even though it means
one of us will have to give up the view."

The front door slammed. "That's my mother," I
said. "She's the only one who slams the door when
she comes in. She keeps forgetting it's heavy."

"Miranda, are you home?"

"Yes, Mother. We're in my room."

I like introducing my mother to somebody new
because she's very nice looking. She has curly red
hair that twists and turns around her face, and
though she's tall, she has good posture. I've noticed
that most tall people slump around, maybe so they
won't stand out. And my mother has a nice smile.
That's how she got the job as personnel director.
When she smiles at you, you feel like doing what she
says.

"Hello," she said when she came to the door.

"Mother, this is Phoebe. Remember I told you I
met a girl in the park last week?" I could tell by the
look in her eyes that she didn't remember but she
smiled anyway.

"Nice to meet you, Phoebe."

"Hello, Mrs. Bartlett."

"Miranda, I forgot to get a vegetable for dinner.

Would you mind going to the fruit stand? I can't face that scene on Broadway again. Just get some green beans and a head of lettuce."

"All right. Want to come, Phoebe?"

"No, I'd better take Dungeon home. He looks as if he might fall asleep right here." The two dogs were curled up on the rug beside each other.

Mother laughed when she looked at them. "Miranda, how convenient to find a friend for yourself and a friend for your dog at the same time."

"River alert," Alex shouted from the hall. We all looked out the window.

"That's beautiful," Phoebe gasped.

It was the *Clearwater,* this old sloop that goes up and down the Hudson to promote cleaning up the river.

"First time we've seen her this spring," Mother said. "That boat always reminds me of one we used to see off the coast in the summers."

"I like your mother," Phoebe said when we got in the elevator. "She seems so young and funny."

"She's all right as mothers go," I said with a grin.

"Do you want to come to my place for dinner tomorrow night? I'm sure my parents would like to meet you. They keep bugging me to make more friends, but I don't like the kids in my school. They have their own little groups. I'm really on my own there."

"Sure. I'd love to come for dinner. What time?"

"Seven. See you then." She started across the street. Then she came back. "One more thing. My parents are very formal. Do you mind wearing a dress?" She looked kind of embarrassed.

"Oh no, that's fine," I said quickly.

"Great. See you tomorrow."

"I saw Margaret in the park this afternoon. She was with her new 'gentleman.' They were holding hands." We were trying to eat dinner quickly because Pops and I were going to a block association meeting at eight thirty.

"What was he like?" Alex asked.

"He's much younger than she is. And very smooth. Buckle loafers and a V-neck sweater. It looks to me like he had his hair done."

"Miranda, you're exaggerating," Pops said.

"He's an actor on the soap operas. He's trying to break into some Broadway shows."

"You certainly got a lot of information out of him," Alex said.

"Just following your example, brother dear." I popped the last piece of cake into my mouth. "Actually, Margaret told me about him when we were up at the zoo last week. Her first younger man."

"Well, if he makes Margaret happy, then I think it's just great," my mother said.

I didn't answer. That sounded nice but somehow I felt left out.

"Ready, Miranda? It's almost eight-thirty." My father stood up. He and I are the ones who go to these meetings. Mother is usually too tired and Alex doesn't care. Pops and I go just to watch the characters. Besides, I like seeing people I know when I walk down the block. The block association turns the block into a little village.

Jack Shirmer was running the meeting. He's pretty good at getting people to agree on something. Or at least to stop talking and vote. The big issue tonight was whether we were going to plant flowers around the trees this spring.

"Last year, somebody stole the ones from around my tree. Made me so mad." That was an older woman who comes to every meeting. I see her a lot out on the block, sitting on a garbage can.

"And the dogs use those places to go to the bathroom," said Mrs. Weiss, this prim old lady from our building.

"We all have to be better about cleaning up after our dogs," Mr. Shirmer said. "I spoke to someone about that just the other morning."

My father raised his hand. "Why don't we put fences around the trees?"

"Costs money, John. And it would take some work."

"But flowers would certainly brighten up the block." That was Margaret talking. I hadn't seen her when we first came in.

The discussion went on like that for a while. Then they moved on to fixing the date for the summer block party. My father agreed to do the signs again. Margaret said she'd run the plant booth, and Mr. Sawyer from our building offered to look into the music possibilities. The meeting broke up pretty early. Pops and I walked to Broadway for an ice cream cone, which is also part of our ritual.

I picked chocolate almond ripple, my all-time favorite, and Pops had strawberry, which he has every time. We walked home slowly, licking the drips and talking.

"How's your friend Katherine? She hasn't come over lately."

"We had a fight. Well, not really a fight, but she started hanging around with Viola Dawson, who is my absolute enemy. Last week when I had asthma at baseball, Viola was playing first base. I came wheezing up, and she looked through me as if I were dead. She's the most selfish girl I've ever met." I finished my tirade and went back to licking the ice cream cone.

"So you've crossed Katherine off your list just because she dared talk to the villainous Viola?"

My father loves to tease me.

"Talk to her? She did more than that. I saw them up at the Bronx Zoo last Saturday, and yesterday I heard them making plans to go to Katherine's apartment after school."

"Oh, yes, that does sound like full-scale treachery," Pops said solemnly.

"So now Margaret's got her young gentleman and Katherine's got Viola and I'm stuck with Frisbee again," I said slowly. I was half joking but only half. "Except for Phoebe."

"Who's Phoebe?"

"She's a girl I met in the park last weekend. She takes care of a dog who looks exactly like Frisbee. These people pay her to take him out for walks. I think it's ridiculous to keep a dog in the city if you're not even going to walk him."

"Where does Phoebe live?"

"Across the street from us. I'm going there for dinner tomorrow night. She asked me to wear a dress since her parents are very formal. That makes me a little nervous."

"I haven't seen you in a dress since you were about six years old." Pops pulled open the door for me.

"Oh, Pops, stop exaggerating." The inner glass door was locked, which meant the night doorman had gone off somewhere.

"Jimmy must be having a cigarette in the basement again," I said.

"Is that what he does? I've always wondered." Pops put the last bite of ice cream in his mouth. "You've got a smudge of ice cream on your chin," he said, wiping it off with his napkin. "We must remove all the evidence." We knew if Alex found out about the ice cream, he would give us a lecture on the preservatives they put in ice cream. Pops and I like our special times together.

# 5 · Dinner at Phoebe's

It took me a long time to get ready to go to Phoebe's. Alex kept knocking on the door and groaning that he had to get in to do his homework, but I didn't pay any attention. The trouble was I really don't wear dresses at all. I have these skinny legs with knobby knees that I don't like very much. So I changed about three times and then ended up wearing the dark blue dress that I had picked out the first time. When I went into my parents' room to look in the mirror, my father was sitting on the bed watching the news. He rolled his eyes and gave me a huge whistle.

"You look terrific, Miranda."

"Oh, stop it, Pops. I do not. Look at those knees."

"Yeah, look at those knees," Alex said. He studied my outfit carefully. "All I can say is I don't think it was worth the two hours you spent to put it together."

I gave him a murderous look and he left. "Sometimes I really can't stand Alex."

"I know, he is irritating. But you've got to learn to just rise above him."

I grinned. "That makes me sound like the table at a seance." I took one last look in the mirror and said good-bye.

"Have a good time," he called.

"Bye, Mother," I said as I went by the kitchen.

"Don't be too late," she said.

When I rang the doorbell, a maid answered the door.

"Is Phoebe here?" I asked.

"Yes, miss. Come in, please."

I couldn't believe my eyes. I was standing in this huge front hall that was about the size of our living room except the ceilings must have been thirteen feet high. There was a portrait of some old person on the wall.

"Hi, Miranda." Phoebe came around the corner. She had on a dress too.

I was glad to see her. The maid and the front hall were making me pretty nervous.

"Come on back to my room."

Phoebe's room had two windows. In front of each one was a little seat where you could curl up with a book or stare at the view of the city. The wallpaper was blue with tiny white curlicues, and the curtains were those floaty white things with ruffles.

"What a fabulous room," I sighed, settling down on her bed. "Those are just the kind of curtains I've always wanted."

"Mother decorated the room," she said with a shrug. "I never pay much attention to things like that."

"Can you see Alex letting me put up those curtains?"

We both laughed at the idea. There was a knock at the door.

"Come in," Phoebe called.

"It's almost time for dinner." Phoebe's mother stepped inside.

"Mom, this is Miranda Bartlett," Phoebe said.

"Hello, Miranda. I'm so pleased to meet you. We were delighted when Phoebe said she had invited you for dinner." She put out her hand and I shook it, feeling a little silly. She was quite short and had very nice blue eyes and blondish hair that was going gray just above her ears. She and Phoebe didn't look at all alike.

"Come in the living room while we have a drink, Phoebe. You know your father likes to have some time with you before dinner."

We trooped down the hall into the living room,

which was about three times the size of ours. Mr. Livingston was sitting in a big easy chair reading the paper. He stood up and shook my hand.

"Nice to meet you, Miranda. Hello, Goose," he said, giving Phoebe a kiss.

"Please don't call me that, Dad. You know I can't stand it." Phoebe flopped down into a chair and put her feet up on a leather stool.

Mr. Livingston smiled at me. "I keep thinking she's still my little girl, but she's growing up fast."

I thought he was cute, but that kind of talk obviously drove Phoebe crazy.

"Cut it out, Dad."

"Phoebe." Mrs. Livingston had a certain tone in her voice that meant don't go too far. There was a small tense silence.

"Where do you go to school, Miranda?" Mr. Livingston asked.

"The Country Day School. I've been going there since first grade. It's over on Ninety-first Street and Madison." I was babbling away out of nervousness.

"Well, that's nice," Mrs. Livingston said. "You can take the bus over like Phoebe."

"We ran into each other on the bus last week," Phoebe said.

"Dinner is served." The maid was gone before I even noticed her.

We sat at the dining room table in front of the window. There were candles and a tablecloth and silverware and linen napkins. The maid served us dinner, which started off with cold soup.

"Tell me about your day at school, Phoebe," her father said. "Did you have that history test you were talking about?"

"Yes."

"How did it go?"

"Awful. The Middle Ages are so boring with those knights and ladies-in-waiting crashing around. Next year I get to drop history. I can't wait."

"I'm not sure that's a good idea, Phoebe. I want you to have a good grounding in history. You will need it later on in life."

"What for?" Phoebe said. She had this kind of grouchy tone in her voice. In fact, she seemed very different around her parents than when she was alone with me.

"It will give you a good starting-off point to look at the history that's going on around you. How politicians operate and whether they are making the right decisions. That sort of thing." Mr. Livingston sat back so the maid could take his soup bowl.

"You live right across the street, Miranda?" Mrs. Livingston said.

"Yes. In 160. We moved there just after my older brother was born."

"They have a great view of the river," Phoebe said. "Right up to the bridge."

The next course was steak with gravy and little pieces of parsley sprinkled over it. I hadn't eaten a steak since Pops took us out to celebrate Alex's birthday last year.

"This looks delicious," I said, taking a big slice.

"It's Phoebe's favorite dinner. We have it every Tuesday night. Save some room, because we finish off with coffee ice cream and chocolate sauce." Mrs. Livingston smiled at her daughter but Phoebe didn't notice. She was busy pouring gravy over her meat.

"Mrs. Whitman, the coach, says they might start up a track and field team next year at school," Phoebe said. "She said I could try out for it even though you're supposed to be in the tenth grade."

"I wish you paid as much attention to your homework as you do to your running, Phoebe. Your grades went down quite a bit on your mid-term report card." Mr. Livingston put his fork and knife together at the edge of the plate. I couldn't believe he had already finished. I was savoring every bite.

"Harold, let's talk about this with Phoebe privately. I don't think it's fair to put Miranda through it," Mrs. Livingston said.

"All right, dear. Sorry, Miranda. Phoebe doesn't have much time for me these days. She's always out in the park doing her mile and a half."

"Two miles, Dad. I'm up to two now," Phoebe said proudly.

"You've got to be careful in that park, Goose. I don't want you running too far or too late at night. You be sure to get in before dark."

"I do, Dad," Phoebe said.

"Phoebe, I'm going to that Manet exhibit on Saturday with your Aunt Grace. Wouldn't you like to come with us? Maybe Miranda could come too."

"Oh, Mom, I hate those museum trips. Anyway, I already promised Mrs. Foster I would baby-sit for her on Saturday morning."

I ate my dessert quickly. I could tell Phoebe really wanted to get away from the table.

"May we please be excused?" Phoebe asked the minute I put down my spoon.

"Yes. Go ahead. But Phoebe, I'd like to talk to you after Miranda has left," her father said.

"Sorry about that dinner, Miranda," Phoebe said when we got back to her room. "They were worse than usual." She threw herself down on her bed. "See what I mean about being the only child? I'm the one thing in life they have to worry about. Sometimes they drive me up the wall."

"That dinner sure tasted great," I said, standing in front of her bookcase. "I haven't had a piece of steak in about a year."

"I've got something to show you," Phoebe said,

coming up beside me. She pulled out a book about running and opened it up to a page that was marked in the corner. "I was thinking about your asthma and running so I looked it up in here. Read what this woman says."

The paragraph said something about the fact it was all right for asthmatics to run as long as they started off slowly, and that it would actually strengthen their lungs. I handed the book back to her.

"Won't you try it? I bet you think you just go out the first day and run until you drop. Well, that's not how you start at all. The first week you walk every day for thirty minutes."

"I already do that with Frisbee."

"I know. That's just what I was thinking. Then the second week, you run until you begin to feel winded and you walk again. You aren't actually running a mile and a half until the eighth week. I bet you could do that."

I looked out the window. "Why do you want me to start running?"

"For the company. It's no fun going out alone every day. Why don't you try it with me tomorrow and if you get asthma, we'll stop."

"All right," I said. I didn't want to sound like a sissy.

"Great." She looked so happy that it worried me.

"I'm never going to be able to keep up with you, Phoebe."

"Stop thinking about it. That's the nice thing about running. You don't have to compete against anybody else. No matter how you do it, you're getting the exercise. Come on over and meet the Fosters. I've got to get Dungeon."

"Does your father let you go out when it's dark?"

Phoebe shrugged. "No. But if I go quietly, he doesn't know about it."

We snuck out of the house and walked across the hall. A young woman came to the door. She was holding a baby.

"Oh, hello, Phoebe." She looked surprised. "Larry just took Dungeon out."

"Oh, I meant to come earlier but we just finished dinner. This is my friend, Miranda. She lives across the street in 160."

"Hello," I said.

Phoebe started tickling the baby under the chin. "Hello, Amy. Isn't she cute, Miranda?"

"How old is she?" I asked.

"Just six months," Mrs. Foster said. "I have to go nurse her now, Phoebe. Thanks for dropping by. And you can still baby-sit for me on Saturday morning?"

"Oh, yes. I thought maybe I could take her out to the park," Phoebe said.

Mrs. Foster looked a little worried. "We'll talk about that. I'm not sure what her schedule will be. Good-bye." She closed the door.

"She sure seemed in a hurry to get rid of us," I said. We were waiting for the elevator to come up.

"She fusses over Amy a lot," said Phoebe. "She picks that baby up the minute she cries."

"I've got Christopher on Saturday morning. Maybe we could go to the playground together," I said slowly.

"That would be great." The elevator came and we both got in. "I'll walk you home," said Phoebe with a grin. "Who's Christopher?"

"He's this three-year-old in our building. I take care of him a lot on the weekends, and his mother's hired me to come every morning for five weeks this summer. If I can stand it."

"What's wrong with him?"

"Nothing really. Except that he got a red plastic motorcycle for his birthday that makes this horrible noise, and he loves to run over my toes with it. Sometimes he takes off down the sidewalk, and I have to run to keep up."

"See, if you start running with me, I'll get you in shape to keep up with Christopher. Let's meet tomorrow in the park at four."

"All right," I said. "Thanks for dinner."

"That's okay. Good-bye."

Alex was still awake when I came in. "How was your date?" he asked. His voice in the dark room made me jump.

"All right. Those people must have a lot of money," I said quietly. "They have a huge apartment and a maid who serves dinner and linen napkins, and we had steak. It was incredible."

"What are Phoebe's parents like?"

I thought for a while before I answered. "They seem kind of stiff. And stuffy. They are older than Mother and Pops. And they fuss a lot over Phoebe. She says it drives her up the wall. She thinks I'm lucky to have you."

"Well, that's another thing she and I agree on," Alex said.

"What was the first thing?" I asked, pulling on my nightgown.

"Exercise."

"Oh, that. Well, for your information, I agreed to try running with her tomorrow afternoon."

"Hey, I want to see that. Where are you meeting?"

"None of your business, you creep. I'm not going to let you sit there and make fun of me."

We were silent for a while.

"I was just kidding, Miranda. I think it's great that you're going to start running," Alex said. He was leaning his head over the edge of the top bunk.

"It will serve you right if I have to be carted away in an ambulance. Pops is the only one who takes my asthma seriously." I turned over on my side and stared at the wall. I closed my eyes and tried not to think about tomorrow. I couldn't tell if I was more scared about getting asthma or looking dumb in front of Phoebe.

## 6 · I Start Running

I was waiting in Riverside Park across the street from our building exactly at four. Phoebe was late, and Frisbee kept tugging on the leash. She couldn't figure out why we were just standing there.

Finally Phoebe came, dressed in running shorts and those blue sneakers. She waved hello and dashed across the street against the light with Dungeon trotting along beside her.

"Let's go down onto the promenade," I said. "Alex said he might come watch, and I don't want him to find us."

"Okay."

Once we were in the park, we stopped at a bench and took the leashes off the dogs.

"First, you warm up," Phoebe explained. "It stretches out your muscles so it won't be a great shock to the system when you suddenly do all that exercise. Lean over and touch your toes." I couldn't get anywhere near them. "No, don't bounce. Just hang there for a full minute. You'll feel everything stretching."

"I also feel the blood rushing to my head," I mumbled.

"That's all right. It's good for the brain cells. Now stand up and put your foot on the bench. Reach your arm over and try to touch your toes. That's fine. It doesn't matter how far you can get. Just stretch it out." I noticed she was holding her foot. "Now the other leg."

I can't believe I'm actually doing this. Just like all the fools I've been laughing at from the bathroom window."

"Last exercise," Phoebe said. "Come over to the tree. I usually do this one in the elevator on my way down because you need a wall. Stand away from the tree. Put your arms out so your palms are flat against it. That's right. Now bend your arms so that your face comes near the tree, but keep your heels on the ground. Straighten your arms out again. Do you feel your calf muscles stretching?"

"Yes," I groaned. "When I'm through with all this, I'll be lucky if I can walk home, much less run anywhere."

"Oh, stop your complaining. It's not that bad."

Phoebe grinned over at me from her tree. "Wait till we move on to sit-ups. Okay, that's enough. Now we can start running."

We started off jogging very slowly, barely more than a walk.

"The whole secret is to keep a rhythm. Sing in your head something like one, two, buckle my shoe. Anything to keep up the same pace. Don't run on your toes. Just put your whole foot down on the ground at once." She sprinted ahead and ran backward for a while, looking at me critically. "Don't flap your arms out to the side so much. Just relax everything. Your arms, your shoulders, your neck, even your face. You look mad enough to kill somebody."

"Yes, you, for getting me into this."

"Don't waste breath talking."

We jogged along for quite a while, and I had to admit that I sort of liked it. I began to do everything naturally without thinking about it. I noticed the trees sailing by and my feet slapping down very evenly and Frisbee running up ahead.

"All right, that's enough for now. We're already up to Ninety-sixth Street. That's eight blocks, so Miranda, the local asthmatic, just ran a little over a quarter of a mile."

When we stopped, I was breathing heavily but no wheezes. I couldn't believe it myself. We walked back down the promenade and ran a little more, from 83rd Street down to 78th, Phoebe talking to me the whole way.

"It's easy to know your distance in the city. Twenty city blocks equals one mile, so by the time we get home we will have covered almost two miles."

"I don't believe it. It doesn't feel that far at all," I said. I slowed down to a walk again. This time I felt wheezier, so we walked home slowly. Alex was down in the lobby, waiting for us.

"I've got the ambulance waiting right out front," he said, jumping up. "Just sit her down here. Bring up the oxygen, boys."

"Oh, shut up," I said, laughing.

"She ran a little over a half mile, all together," Phoebe said proudly. "We're going out again tomorrow."

"Good heavens, it's Marathon Miranda," Alex exclaimed, clapping his hand to his forehead. Sometimes he is just ridiculous.

We went out every afternoon that week, and I began to look forward to the routine.

"I can see why people get hooked on this," I said to Phoebe as we were walking home Friday afternoon. "You're bumping along at this nice even pace and suddenly your mind starts to travel and think about all sorts of things and before you know it, you've made it past the tree you couldn't reach the day before."

"And you haven't had any asthma at all," said Phoebe.

"The weather's been very clear," I said quickly. "It's the heat and pollution that really get to me. Wait until the middle of the summer."

"Doomsday Miranda," she said. "You always look at the grim side of things. Aren't you proud of yourself for how much you've done so far? I think you're terrific. I thought we were going to be doing an eighth of a mile for the next two weeks."

"I guess so," I said with a smile. "I just don't like to count on anything. Then I won't be disappointed."

"Are we still meeting in the playground tomorrow? Mrs. Foster wants me to baby-sit from nine until twelve."

"Fine. Let's meet down in your lobby at ten. Did she say you could take Amy out?" I asked.

"Not yet. But I'm sure I'll be able to convince her. Mrs. Foster really likes me. See you."

This time Phoebe was waiting for me when I arrived. Getting Christopher and his motorcycle into the elevator was always a problem because he liked to hold the elevator button and ride the motorcycle at the same time.

"Where have you been? This baby's been screaming solidly since nine o'clock." Phoebe groaned. "I hope the fresh air puts her to sleep." I looked in at Amy who was red-faced and still yelling.

"Have you tried flipping her onto her stomach?" I asked. "Maybe she has a bubble."

"I walked her around on my shoulder for an hour already, but I'll try anything." She turned Amy over, and the baby went to sleep.

"The magic touch," I said with a grin.

"I wish you'd come a little earlier," Phoebe said grumpily.

There were a lot of people in the playground. We tied Frisbee and Dungeon to the fence.

"Mrs. Foster says Dungeon slipped out of that collar yesterday," Phoebe said. "I hope he doesn't do it again."

I couldn't answer because Christopher was already off on a wild rampage. For the first fifteen minutes at the playground, he just tears around and around the benches on his motorcycle, knocking over everything. I find the whole thing very irritating. I flail along in his path, picking up small children and toys and apologizing to everybody.

I didn't see Phoebe to talk to again for half an hour. Finally, I had Christopher settled quietly in the sandbox. Phoebe came over, pushing the carriage.

"You look exhausted," she said.

"Wouldn't you? Have you been watching me?" I was jealous of her baby-sitting job. Amy was still asleep. I noticed Phoebe wasn't listening to me.

"Dungeon's gone," she said suddenly in a horrified voice. "He must have slipped off his leash." She left the carriage and ran for the fence, calling Dungeon. Just at that moment there was a terrible commotion on the other side of the playground. Two dogs were fighting, and some lady was screaming that her child was going to be bitten. Phoebe ran by me again yelling that it was Dungeon.

"Christopher, you stay right here in this sandbox. Don't move," I warned. I put the brake on the carriage and ran with Christopher's plastic bucket to the water fountain. My father always told me to pour cold water over fighting dogs. By the time the bucket was filled, the racket had stopped. I went over anyway. The dogs were separated but still snarling at each other. Phoebe was trying to pull Dungeon away. The dog was bleeding from his lip.

"Here, give him some water," I said, putting down the bucket.

"That collie's mean," Phoebe said in a low voice. "I've seen her in the park before."

"I've got to get back to Christopher," I said. "Bring the bucket."

"I'm coming too."

My heart dropped to my feet when I looked at the

sandbox. There was his truck and his shovel. But no Christopher and no motorcycle. I looked around the playground. No kids were riding motorcycles, and I couldn't see anyone with a red shirt on.

Phoebe came up beside me. "Where's Christopher?" she asked.

"I don't know. He's gone. I can't see him anywhere."

"Wait a minute. Let me tie up Dungeon again, and I'll help you look."

By the time she came back, I was sure he wasn't in the playground. "Take the carriage over to that lady by the swings and ask her to look after Amy," I said to Phoebe. "Then you go up the hill toward the monument, and I'll take the path by the cherry trees. Ask everyone if they've seen him. He couldn't have gone far."

I ran off down the path, calling Christopher's name. By the time I got to the river and was starting back, I was completely panicked. What if he hadn't gone this way? What if he was trying to cross Riverside Drive? What would I tell his mother?

Phoebe and I met by the entrance to the playground.

"No sign of him up there," she said.

"What if he went up to the Drive?" I yelled.

"Calm down, Miranda, we'll find him. He wouldn't

have gone up that big hill. He couldn't have made it on the motorcycle."

"Maybe he's been kidnapped. Remember that weird man that was sitting on the bench near the sandbox?" I was beginning to fall apart.

"Let's check the playground again, and then I'll go down to the promenade and you take the road to the tennis courts." We walked around the playground asking people if they had seen a little boy in a red shirt on a motorcycle.

"I remember him. Isn't he the one who knocked over my little girl?" one woman asked. "I thought I saw him heading for the water fountain."

"Of course," I said to Phoebe. "He would have been following me when I went to fill the bucket." We both started racing up the path. By this time, he had been gone for about twenty minutes, and I was sure he was dead.

Suddenly Phoebe pulled me to a stop. "Look over there," she said, pointing at the wall of the promenade. There was Christopher, sitting on his motorcycle staring up at an ice cream vendor who was handing out popsicles.

"Christopher," I yelled as I started to run. Well, of course he thought I was playing a game with him, and he turned around and pushed off on his motorcycle. By the time I caught up with him, I wasn't sure whether I wanted to hug him or murder him.

We collected Amy, who was still sleeping, and the two dogs and plodded slowly back up the hill.

"I'm wiped out," I said to Phoebe. "I kept thinking about how his mother would look if I had really lost him."

"Next time, we'd better leave the dogs home. The whole thing was Dungeon's fault. Do you want to run this afternoon?" she asked.

"Are you kidding? I'm going to bed for the rest of the day."

# 7 • Tea at Margaret's

When school got out the next week, Phoebe and I
started jogging every afternoon. After three weeks,
I could run three-quarters of a mile without stopping
to rest. I couldn't believe it and neither could the
family.

"Are you sure that's good for your asthma?" my
father asked one morning at breakfast.

"She hasn't wheezed once at night since she
started," Alex said. "If you had just followed my ad-
vice years ago, my dear—"

"Alex, that's enough," Pops said. "I think it's terrific you are running, Miranda, but I want you to be
careful with the hot weather coming on."

"At least the pollution isn't too bad along the

river," I said. "And I usually remember to take the inhaler, just in case."

"Phoebe wants her to run in the Central Park marathon in September," said Alex. I made a face at him. Alex deserves the nosy brother of the month award. How did he know that anyway?

"How long is it?" my mother asked.

"Six point two miles. Don't worry, I'll never be running that far." Secretly, I was hoping I could do it.

"What do you want for your birthday, Miranda? It's Friday, isn't it?" Mother asked.

"Yes, it is. I don't know. Another pair of jeans, I guess." I really wanted running shoes, but I'd already been down to the store to look at them, and I knew they cost thirty dollars. That was much more than my parents usually spend, so I'd decided to save my baby-sitting money for them. Phoebe was bugging me about running in sneakers. She said it was going to give me runner's knee and several other terrible-sounding diseases. I'd already felt a few twinges in my knee, but I didn't tell anybody about them. It would be hard to explain to Phoebe that thirty dollars was a lot of money for my parents to spend on something like shoes.

"Get her a pretty dress, Virginia," my father said. He winked at me. "She'll need another one if she goes out calling again."

"Do you want to ask Phoebe for dinner that night?"

"Yes, Mother. That would be fun." I stood up and started to clear the plates. "Margaret has asked me for tea with Phoebe on Thursday. I hope she doesn't have her man with her. I don't like him very much."

"Now, Miranda, give him a chance," Pops said. "If he makes Margaret happy, there must be something good about him."

"When we met in the elevator last week, he went right on looking at himself in the corner mirror while he was talking to me," I said. "I wonder if all actors are that vain."

He was at tea. I saw his fancy loafer swinging back and forth at the bottom of his leg the minute we stepped in the door.

"Steven was able to come too," Margaret said with a smile. I think she could tell I wasn't too happy about it.

"Margaret, this is Phoebe Livingston and this is Mr. Delaney."

"Nice to meet you, Phoebe." We sat down and Margaret put on the kettle.

"Miranda told me you were an actor," Phoebe said. "What kind of acting do you do?"

"Some television. Some big summer theaters. I'll be up in Boothbay, Maine, in August."

I went over to help Margaret pour the tea, but she shooed me away. "Go talk to Steven. He likes to be surrounded by pretty women."

He was still talking. "I've had a few small parts in afternoon soap operas. In fact, I just finished a job last week. They killed me off," he said with a smile.

"I'm delighted," Margaret said as she came in carrying the teapot. "It means I can see more of you. When Steven is working hard, I don't hear from him for days." They smiled at each other, and I shifted nervously in my seat. The next trip, Margaret carried in a huge vanilla cake, and they all sang happy birthday, which made me blush.

"I actually baked this cake, Miranda," Margaret said. "You can tell because it's very lopsided."

"It looks beautiful to me," Steven said.

"Miranda, stop staring at it and cut it," said Phoebe with a grin. "I'm starved."

Margaret laughed. "Ah, Miranda, I see you have found us a true soul mate. A fellow traveler to the land of Baskin-Robbins' chocolate almond ripple."

"And away from Alex," I muttered as I cut the first piece.

"Miranda's brother is a health food nut," Margaret said to Steven. "He's forever accosting us in the elevator, delivering lectures on the evils of sugar and the importance of bran in your diet."

We ate for a while in silence. Margaret gave me my present, which was a small soapstone box with a whale carved on the top.

"It's the one we saw up at the zoo," I said with a smile. "Thank you." She came over and gave me a hug. She's like that. Very mushy. Always has been. She's the only person I don't mind hugging me. Besides my parents, who don't do it very often.

"You certainly do like plants," Phoebe said. Margaret had sat down on the couch again next to Steven. I saw her put her hand on his knee.

"You think this is bad," I said quickly. "You should see her bedroom."

"Go ahead," Margaret said.

I showed Phoebe the pictures on the bureau. I noticed there was one of Steven now stuck in the corner of the mirror.

"Who's this?" Phoebe asked. She was pointing to an old picture of a little boy.

I picked it up and looked at it carefully. He was dressed in a baggy pair of shorts and sneakers.

"I don't know. I've never seen this picture before. I'll have to ask Margaret."

"Look at this weird hand," Phoebe said, peering through the glass case.

"That's the mummy's hand she got on her trip to Egypt," I said. "Margaret used to work for a travel magazine. They sent her all around the world."

"I think she's neat," Phoebe whispered. "And she's so pretty."

We went back to the living room. Margaret and Steven were sitting even closer together, laughing over something.

"We've got to go," I said. "I have to walk Frisbee. Thank you, Margaret, for the cake and the box. Everything was great."

Margaret walked us to the door. "I'm glad I finally met you, Phoebe. Miranda has told me about your running. In fact, I saw you two out there one afternoon last week. You looked very serious."

"Oh, we are. We're going into a marathon in September," Phoebe said brightly. "You'll have to come watch us."

"I will," Margaret said. "See you later."

"I wish you wouldn't tell everybody that," I said to Phoebe as we were waiting for the elevator. "I'll never be running six miles by September."

"Don't be so negative, Miranda. Look how well you've done already. And no asthma at all." She gave me this funny smile. "Sometimes I wonder if you make up that asthma story to get out of things."

I was furious. But I knew if I got too mad it would sound fake, so I just shrugged. "Ask Alex," I said. "He's the one who has to sleep through my wheezing every night."

The elevator came and we got inside. Phoebe pushed seven.

"I'll come up with you to get Frisbee."

I didn't say anything. Sometimes Phoebe seems very dense to me. Didn't she know what a mean thing she'd said? I turned away and stood waiting for the door to open.

"I like Margaret's friend, Steven. What do you think of him?"

"Not much," I said.

"I think it would be romantic to go out with an actor. Daddy says his father wanted to be an actor but never made it and ended up selling typewriters instead."

Alex was home. Phoebe went back into our room to talk to him while I looked for Frisbee's leash. When she came out she had this little smile on her face.

"Wait till you see what you're getting for your birthday," she said. "Alex and I have been doing some plotting."

"Hey, Phoebe, be quiet," Alex called from the room. "You're going to give everything away."

"I'd better go get Dungeon," she said. "Mrs. Foster is making me write down the times I take him out in a little book. I think she doesn't trust me anymore or something."

I didn't say anything. I was still mad about what

she'd said about my asthma. Alex was always accusing me of making it up so I wouldn't have to try things. He used to say it came from my fear of failing. Bunch of hogwash he read in one of those psychology books of his.

They gave me running shoes. I couldn't believe it when I opened the box. Bright blue ones just like Phoebe's.

"You can take them back if they don't fit," Phoebe said. "I took one of your sneakers to the store and they gave me the size closest to it."

"We all chipped in," Mother said with a smile. "It's your only present from us, dear."

"Oh, it's the best present of all," I said. And they were beautiful. I walked around the living room staring at my feet. My bright blue feet.

"If you keep walking around with your eyes on the ground, you're going to bump into something and hurt yourself, Miranda."

"But aren't they beautiful, Mother?"

My mother looked solemnly down at my shoes. She takes my questions very seriously.

"No," she said slowly. "I don't really think they're beautiful. But if they make your feet happy, then I'm glad we got them for you."

"I have another present for you, Miranda," Phoebe said. She handed me a square package, all wrapped up. It was the book about running that she'd shown me after dinner that night. Inside the flap, it said, "To Marathon Miranda from Phoebe, the huffer and puffer."

"Very funny," I said. "It's really the other way around."

"Let's all go walk off some of this cake," Pops said. He loves to go out for a walk in the park after dinner.

Phoebe and I fell back behind the others. Alex and Mother were having an argument about some constellation.

"Thanks for the book," I said.

"You're welcome. It's not much of a present but it's fun to read. She even has a chapter on what to think about when you're running."

We were both silent for a minute. I wanted to tell her why I had been mad before.

"It makes me mad when you say I don't have asthma," I said slowly. "I'm not a joker."

She glanced at me. "Sorry. I didn't really mean it." Then she looked hurt, and I felt bad.

"I guess you've never seen me have an attack," I muttered.

"I hope I never do," Phoebe answered.

# 8 · My Big Attack

I think it was the week after my birthday that I got
the attack. It gets pretty hot in New York in the
summer, and sometimes the end of June can feel like
August. I remember we didn't run at all for two days
in a row. The third day Phoebe called and said we
had to go out or our muscles would turn to mush.

"In two days?" I said.

"Miranda, it's already the end of June, and I'm
leaving for Connecticut in a couple of weeks. Then
you're going to Vermont, and the marathon is right
after we get back. No time to spare." She lowered
her voice. "Besides my mother is driving me up the
wall about cleaning my room. I've got to get out of
here."

The lobby downstairs was cool, but when I walked

out to the street the heat almost knocked me over. Phoebe met me at the corner.

"I can't run two feet in this weather," I gasped.

"It's not as bad as yesterday," she said as we waited for the light.

I realized I'd forgotten my inhaler. "I'd better go back," I said. "I forgot my medicine."

"Oh, come on, Miranda, we won't go that far. Let's just get running." She sprinted across the street against the light. I joined her on the other side, and we headed south along the drive. The first ten blocks are downhill so I trotted along without too much trouble, but by the time we hit 79th Street and started up the rise by the playground, I could feel my chest starting to close up. I slowed down a bit and tried to breathe more deeply.

"Come on, Miranda, keep up the pace," Phoebe said.

"I'm starting to wheeze," I said.

She didn't answer but there was this little look on her face as if to say, not that again. It made me furious. I speeded up and passed her. By the time we reached 75th Street I felt as if my chest were going to cave in but I kept at it, my feet pounding down, counting numbers in my head over and over.

Phoebe caught up with me. "Miranda, slow down, you sound terrible."

"It's nothing," I gasped. "Just a little asthma. Don't

lose the pace, Phoebe. We mustn't let our muscles turn to mush."

"Miranda, please stop," she said, grabbing my arm.

I shook her off and kept on going. My legs were starting to tremble, and I was sweating all over. The next time she tried to stop me, I slowed down. We walked along while I tried to catch my breath but the wheezing kept getting worse. I felt as if I were pulling the air in through six layers of cheesecloth.

Phoebe led me to a bench by the river, and we sat down. My asthma attacks are pretty scary to listen to, especially if you've never heard one before. They still scare me sometimes, but the worst part is looking at the other person's face. Phoebe looked awful.

"I should get home," I gasped. "It's just going to get worse."

Some people were starting to gather around. That always makes me nervous. I'm sort of claustrophobic, especially when I can't breathe very well to begin with.

We started to walk home but I had to stop a lot to catch my breath, and I guess Phoebe panicked. She told some man I needed help, and before I knew it, this police car was screaming down the promenade with everybody jumping out of the way. They put me in the back seat, and one policeman tried to make me lie down, which is the worst thing for asthma.

"Phoebe, just get them to take me home. I don't want to go to any hospital."

"Officer, she has some medicine at home. If you could just take her there, please," Phoebe said.

"She sounds pretty bad to me. We're going into Roosevelt Hospital. They'll give her oxygen."

I started to cry because all I wanted to do was go home and, of course, the crying made my wheezing worse. Phoebe kept patting my shoulder and looking miserable.

In the emergency room, the doctor gave me an adrenalin shot, which clears the whole thing up pretty fast. They called my father, and he came down with Alex to get me. By that time, Phoebe was crying. After we got home, Alex walked across the street with her. When he came back, he sat down beside me on the bed.

"How's Phoebe?" I asked.

"Pretty upset. I guess she's never heard an asthma attack before. She thinks it was all her fault."

I turned over on my side and stared at the wall. I felt miserable. If I hadn't gotten so mad, I would have just stopped running when I started to wheeze, the way I should have. But I knew why I'd done it. I wanted to prove to her that I really did have asthma.

"She's worried that you shouldn't run anymore," Alex said slowly.

I sat up. "But, that's crazy. It was only this one

time, and the weather was terrible, and I didn't have my inhaler."

Alex grinned. "That's what I told her. You weren't going to give up any marathon because of one silly asthma attack."

Just then the doorbell rang. Alex went to answer it and came back with Phoebe. She was carrying a bag from Baskin-Robbins.

"How are you feeling?" she asked shyly.

"I'm fine now," I said. "That adrenalin shot always clears things up right away."

"I brought you a present. Chocolate almond ripple."

"Thanks."

"I remembered it was your favorite from your birthday party."

"I'll get some spoons," Alex said. Which was pretty nice, considering his attitude toward ice cream.

As soon as he was out of the room, Phoebe and I started talking at once. Then we both stopped.

"That attack was all my fault," she said. "I just kept pushing you, and I wouldn't let you go up to get your medicine."

"Don't be ridiculous," I said quickly. "I could have stopped running a lot sooner. I knew just what I was doing." I shrugged. "I just wanted to prove to you that I really do have asthma."

"Don't worry, I believe you," said Phoebe with a

grin. "I'll never doubt you again."

Alex came back in, and we dove into the ice cream. He sat over on the radiator and watched us.

"Mmm, it's good," Phoebe said. "Want some, Alex?"

He did look a little tempted, but he shook his head. "No thanks, I'd rather not rot out my stomach at such a tender age."

"See you tomorrow at four?" I asked just as Phoebe was leaving. "Regular place?"

"Hey, Miranda, I'm not sure you should run anymore. Another attack like that might do you in."

"Are you kidding, Phoebe Livingston? I'm not going to stop now after all these weeks of practice. My muscles would turn to mush by Friday."

Phoebe rolled her eyeballs. "Oh, I wish I'd never said that."

"And what about running improving my lung capacity? You're not going to give up on me just because of one stupid little asthma attack? Nice friend."

"All right, all right. Tomorrow at four." She started out the door. "But please remember your medicine," she called back at me from the hall.

Alex put the rest of the ice cream in the freezer. When he came back, he sat down on the radiator and stared at me with this certain look on his face. I know that look. It means he's about to make one of his great psychological pronouncements.

"Yes, Dr. Bartlett?" I said.

"Amazing," he said solemnly. "Do you realize this is the first time the asthma got in your way?"

"What are you talking about?"

"Well, before you've always used it to get out of things like baseball practice and Viola Dawson's birthday party—"

"I did not!"

"—but this time you're not going to let it stop you from running, no matter what." He nodded his head solemnly. "Yes, Miss Bartlett, I do believe you are improving. The day may come when you'll be able to face the world without my constant attention and assistance."

He ducked, and the pillow I threw from my bed missed him by inches and knocked some books off his desk.

"Good, Miss Bartlett," he said, backing out of the room. By that time I had gotten the pillow from his bed. "I'm glad to see you acting out your aggressions. That's another sign of your good health." He slammed the door behind him, and the second pillow fell into the corner.

"You big creep," I yelled as I crawled back into bed. But the more I thought about it, the more I realized he might be right.

The weather had cooled off by the next day, but Phoebe made me run very slowly. We only did two miles, even though I'd gotten up to two and a half the week before. When I slowed down to a walk, I waved her on. She was up to four miles by now. "Keep going. I'll meet you at the top of the hill at Eighty-seventh Street."

She nodded and trotted on. "I'll take the dogs," she called and whistled for them.

I took one big whiff of my medicine and headed to the path by the river. There were a lot of people walking their dogs and running and pushing baby carriages. I stopped to watch a big freighter coming down the river from the bridge. Suddenly, out of the corner of my eye, I saw someone familiar. Steven Delaney was sitting on a park bench, talking very earnestly to some girl. It was definitely not Margaret. I stood very still watching them because I didn't want him to see me. She must have told him some joke because he leaned back and laughed in this big hearty way, and she kept looking at him with this adoring look as if he were God's gift to women. Blech! After a while, I turned and walked quickly in the opposite direction to be sure they didn't see me.

Phoebe was waiting for me. "Are you all right?" she called when she saw me coming. "I was sure you'd had another attack."

"I saw Steven Delaney with some younger woman. Very pretty. Long blond hair and skinny legs. And they were giggling over something."

"Maybe it's just some fellow actress," Phoebe said.

"Come here, Dungeon," she called.

I snapped the leash on Frisbee and started for home. "Well, they were being very intimate fellow workers," I muttered.

"Want to come up?" Phoebe asked when we got to her building.

"No, thanks. I'm going to stop in and see Margaret."

"All right. Don't forget next Tuesday night. Mother said we could go to a movie." It was Phoebe's thirteenth birthday, and I was going over to the Livingstons' for dinner again.

"Fine. See you tomorrow," I said.

# 9 · My Terrific Idea

I didn't know what I was going to say to Margaret. I hadn't seen her since my birthday tea, and I didn't want to walk in and say, "Hey, I just saw Steven in the park with some girl."

She was wearing her bathrobe when she opened the door. I've never seen Margaret in a bathrobe. Especially at five o'clock in the afternoon.

"Hi, Margaret. How are you?"

"Hello, Miranda," she said with a tired smile. "Come on in."

"Maybe this isn't a good time. I just haven't seen you in ages."

"I know. I've been hibernating. Would you like some iced tea? Sorry, there's nothing else. I don't think I've even got a cookie in the house."

"You sit down," I said. "I'll get everything." I took two glasses out of the cupboard and opened the refrigerator. "Are you feeling all right?"

"Why do you ask?"

I shrugged. "You look a little tired."

She took the tea without answering. "How's the running?" she said after a while. "It must be bad in this weather."

"I did get asthma yesterday. Poor Phoebe almost passed out when she heard me wheezing." I babbled on, telling her about Roosevelt Hospital and the chocolate almond ripple ice cream. She smiled once but didn't really seem to be listening.

I put down my glass of tea and noticed the picture of the little boy that had been stuck in Margaret's mirror the last time I was there. It was lying on the table beside me.

"Who's this, Margaret?" I asked, holding up the photograph.

Margaret took the picture from me and studied it closely.

"That's James. He was a little boy that my husband and I adopted after we found out I couldn't have children."

"Where is he now?" I asked softly.

"He died when he was five years old," she said. "It

turned out he had a disease from birth. Something that runs in the family. We never knew until it was too late to do anything about it."

"How sad," I said.

"I got out this picture because his face reminded me of Steven's for some reason. But now that I look at it again I don't see any resemblance."

"How is Steven?" I asked.

She shrugged. "Don't ask me. I haven't heard from him since the day after you were here." She got this sort of tight look on her face as if she wanted to stop herself from crying. "We went out that evening with another couple. A friend of Steven's and his girl. Very pretty young thing." I hadn't heard that sarcastic tone in Margaret's voice before. "They live up on Riverside and Ninety-fourth actually. Steven was quite taken with her. The other man and I were left staring at the two of them and feeling like perfect fools."

She stood up and walked into the kitchen. "I guess my age caught up with me this time," she said in this low sad voice.

I went over and threw my arms around her.

"Oh, Margaret, don't say that," I said softly.

"You're nice to drop by, Miranda. I think I'll just go lie down now," she said, patting me on the arm. When she went out of the room, I could see she was crying. I washed the glasses and closed the front door quietly behind me.

I told my parents about Margaret over dinner.

"Poor Margaret," Mother said quietly. "I think she cared more about this Steven than the others."

"What a horrible person," I sputtered. "I bet he's been fooling around with Margaret until something more interesting came along. I hate him."

"Now, Phoebe," Mother said. She doesn't like us to say we hate people.

"I don't like to change the subject," Pops said, "but before I forget, your father called tonight, Virginia. He'd like to know when we're coming to Vermont."

"I told him already," Mother said. "I'm afraid he's getting a little forgetful. The afternoon of the first."

Suddenly I had a terrific idea. "Why don't we ask Margaret to go with us?" I said. "It would be the perfect way for her to forget about that man."

Everybody stopped talking and stared at me.

"She could stay in the cottage."

"That means Alex and you would have to share a room in the big house," Mother said, looking at me in surprise.

Grandpa had a little cottage across the road from the main house, and every summer Alex and I switched off so that he got it one year and I got it the next. It was the only time the whole year that Alex and I could each have our own room. Of course next year that would change if we put up the partition in our room. I loved having that little house in Vermont to myself. It had only one bedroom and a bathroom but it was all mine, separate from everybody else.

"I don't mind sharing with Alex," I said slowly. I knew he'd be mad.

"Oh, no," he groaned. "Miranda and I have to be in together? Why don't we put Margaret in the upstairs room with Miranda and I'll take the cottage?"

We sat and thought about that. I wouldn't mind it if Margaret didn't. It would be fun to have a female roommate for a change.

"Wait a minute, everybody," my father said. "We haven't talked to your grandfather yet, and we haven't even asked Margaret if she wants to come. We can worry about the rooms later."

My mother called Grandpa the next morning before she left for work. He said it was fine with him.

"I'll stop by Margaret's this morning on my way to Broadway," I said. I was planning to go to Woolworth's to look for a birthday present for Phoebe.

"Now, don't push her too hard," my mother said as she headed out the door. "You know how Margaret treasures her privacy. She may prefer to be alone."

Margaret looked a little better when she opened the door but she was still in her robe.

"It's me again but I'm not staying," I said quickly.

"I just want to ask you something."

"Yes?"

"Well, we were all wondering if you'd come to Vermont with us on the first of August. We're going to Grandpa's for our summer visit. We called him last night, and he said he'd love to have you."

"Miranda, what a nice invitation." She smiled, and for a minute she looked like her old self. "Are you sure there'd be room for me? I don't like to get into anybody's way."

"Oh, yes, there's a separate cottage you could stay in or you could share a bedroom with me." She looked a little worried. "Oh, that would be great for me," I said quickly. "Anything would be great after Alex day in and day out."

"At least I don't lift weights," she said with a grin. "Well, I'll think about it and let you know tomorrow. Is that soon enough?"

I nodded but I must have seemed disappointed. I was sure she'd say yes immediately since I was so carried away by the idea.

"It's wonderful of you all to ask me. Thank your mother for me, will you?"

"There are thousands of plants up there, Margaret. You know it's in the country, and there are some great trails through the woods and you could do some bird-watching."

She laughed at me. "I'm sure it's a terrific place, Miranda."

"All right, I'll stop. Mother said not to pressure you." I turned to go. "I'm going to Woolworth's to buy Phoebe a birthday present. Want to come?"

She shook her head. "Not today. But thanks anyway."

All the way down Broadway, I ran over the conversation in my mind, trying to decide whether she'd come or not. By the time I got to Woolworth's I still couldn't decide so I concentrated on Phoebe's present instead.

I think I could live in a dimestore. When I was younger, Alex and I stopped by on the way home from school at least twice a week. We'd cruise the aisles, checking out the new stuff. The clerks always watched us suspiciously. I'm sure they thought we wanted to steal something.

It took me a long time to decide exactly what to get her. Phoebe has everything, and if she doesn't she can get it from her parents, or go buy it herself. Finally I decided on this miniature house. When you looked in the back there were tiny people in every room and tiny pieces of furniture. It sounds like a crazy present but I loved it, and my mother says the best present to buy someone else is the thing you want most for yourself.

I waited until four-thirty that afternoon on the corner but Phoebe never came, so I went over and rang the Livingston apartment on the intercom. After a long time, Phoebe's mother answered.

"Mrs. Livingston, it's Miranda Bartlett. Phoebe was supposed to meet me to go running but she hasn't come. Have you seen her?"

"Miranda, Phoebe's not feeling very well. I'm afraid she won't be able to come down. I'll have her call you tomorrow."

"What's wrong with her?" I said but by that time Mrs. Livingston had hung up.

"She's sick," I said to Frisbee as we trotted off together. "Guess we've got to run it alone today."

That was one of those afternoons when everything seemed to fall into place. When you first start running, your body feels kind of clunky. Your knees crack and your arms feel stiff and your feet hit the ground like two bombs. But then slowly it stops creaking and the gears turn the right way and you run along thinking about the summer trees and the funny way that bird is sitting in that tree and what your good friend could possibly be sick with. And you might as well be sailing because your body isn't bothering you at all. On afternoons like that, I can really see what Phoebe means when she says running helps her think. You're out there in the middle of the biggest city in the world but you're really alone in your own private space.

By the time I got home, I'd run three miles without stopping. Maybe I'd finish that marathon after all.

"Did Phoebe call?" I asked Alex when I got in.

"No. But Margaret left you this note."

It read, "Dear Miranda, I would love to come to Vermont. I've decided it would be the best thing for me and you are wonderful to have asked me. I'll call you tonight. Love, Margaret."

"She's coming," I said to Alex. "I hope she likes it."

"I hope she likes having you as a roommate. See you later. Mother just called to say the Kleins are coming for dinner so I'm going to Peter's."

"Traitor," I muttered. "Phoebe's sick so I can't hide out over there."

Mrs. Klein is one of those people who talks about her miniature poodles and her darling granddaughter all night. She drives the rest of us up a wall, especially my father, but Mr. Klein gives Pops a lot of work so Mother has them over for dinner occasionally.

I called Phoebe that evening but the maid answered and said she was asleep.

"What's wrong with her?" I asked.

"Excuse me, miss?"

"Is she sick?"

"No, I don't think so. I think she's just sleeping."

"How strange," I said when I hung up the phone. Pops was doing the dishes. The Kleins had finally left.

"What's strange?" he asked.

"Phoebe didn't come running today because she was sick. At least that's what her mother told me, but now the maid says she's not sick, she's just sleeping." I picked up a dish towel and started to dry a plate absentmindedly. "Why would Phoebe be sleeping at eight o'clock in the evening?"

"Beats me. Maybe she really is sick but the maid doesn't know it." Pops pulled the drain out of the sink. "Right now, I wouldn't mind having a maid. Or at least a dishwasher."

"I agree. If I had a million dollars, I'd get my own room. How about you, Pops?" This is one of our favorite games. What we would do if we were rich.

"An apartment that was big enough so I could work at home in a high-ceilinged studio that faced north up the river. The perfect light and view for the artist. Then a shack in the country so I could have that garden I used to plant every spring when I was home in Maryland. And a dishwasher." He grinned. "Maybe we'll get the dishwasher."

"My room would have my own old-fashioned desk so I don't have to do my homework on the bed anymore. And two windows so it's not too hot in the summer. Then I'd like a bicycle that's my size. The one I have is about perfect for an eight-year-old. And enough money so I wouldn't have to baby-sit for Christopher ever again."

We put away the dish towels. "Your mother told me that Margaret's coming up to Vermont. That will be fun. I think your grandfather will enjoy her."

"Me too," I said. "Goodnight, Pops." My mind had already started wandering back to Phoebe's strange illness.

## 10 • Phoebe's Big Secret

Believe it or not, I did not see Phoebe again for a week. Every time I called, her mother made some excuse about her not being able to come to the phone, and after a while she began to sound annoyed. She didn't even tell me not to come to dinner on Tuesday. Alex said I should just show up but I didn't have the nerve. Besides, I was getting hurt that Phoebe hadn't called me. Whatever had happened to her couldn't be that bad. Maybe she wasn't as good a friend as I thought.

Margaret seemed better. The day after I got her note, she rang our doorbell.

"Come in, Margaret," I heard my mother say. "We're all delighted you're coming to Vermont with us."

"Well, it's a treat for me," said Margaret. She gave Mother this little hug. "I seem to need a change this year more than ever."

"Do you want some dessert with us?" Pops asked, coming out to greet her. "It's fruit. Alex's night to fix dessert."

Margaret laughed. "Well, I can stomach a little fruit now and then. I'd love some."

She sat down, and Alex gave her a plate. "I'm actually here on business," said Margaret. "Saturday is the block fair, and I'm very late getting organized about it. I've done the calling to get the plants donated but I need some help picking them up, and I also need someone to help me staff the booth on Saturday. Any volunteers?"

"I'll do it," I said quickly. "Christopher's away this week, so I don't have to baby-sit."

"Terrific," Margaret said. "And what about your friend Phoebe? Do you think you could enlist her?"

There was a little silence. "I'll ask her," I said quietly. "She's been pretty busy these days."

"Whatever," Margaret said. "If she can't come, we'll be able to manage. These peaches are delicious."

"I got them at the farmers' market," Alex said. "I went this morning. They have local New Jersey produce. Fresh eggs and bushels of tomatoes and big green salad-bowl lettuce."

"I've heard about that place," Margaret said. "I'll have to try it."

Alex beamed. He'd been raving about that stupid farmers' market all day.

"Come down around ten tomorrow, Miranda," Margaret said as she left. "And bring your mother's grocery cart if you can."

"She certainly seems back to her old self," Mother said as she came in the kitchen.

"That's great," Pops said. "She's a marvelous woman."

Working for Margaret helped me forget about Phoebe. Margaret kept me so busy I couldn't think about anything else. For two days, we went to the local stores and collected plants. Then we took them to Mrs. Flanagan's basement. Poor Mrs. Flanagan! It looked as if all the equipment for the block fair was being stored in her basement.

"You mean we have to come here Saturday morning and take these plants out again?" I asked. There was a sort of desperate tone in my voice.

"That's right. But it won't be bad. I've arranged it so the plant booth will be put in front of this house. We can get people to help us. I think there's a set-up committee." Margaret folded her cart and started back up the stairs. "One more trip to Royal's Florist, and then we have to get working in my place."

"What do we have to do there?"

"Plant some of the cuttings I've started in water and write price tags." She smiled down at me. "See, Miranda, I really couldn't have done this without you."

I looked up and recognized the woman walking toward us. It was Phoebe's mother.

"Hello, Mrs. Livingston," I said, stepping into her path.

"Oh, hello," she said. She gave me a vague smile and kept walking.

"I hope Phoebe's feeling better," I called after her. She didn't answer.

"She seemed to be in a hurry," Margaret said. "What's wrong with Phoebe?"

"I don't know. Every time I call her, the maid says she can't come to the phone or her mother says she's sick. Alex says they're keeping her prisoner in her room." I laughed. "He has a vivid imagination. But the whole thing's a bit mysterious."

"And she never called back?"

I shook my head. "I'm getting a little hurt. I thought we were good friends. No matter what happened to me, I think I'd tell her about it."

"Give her some time, Miranda. There may be a perfectly good explanation."

They predicted rain for the day of the fair but the weather was fine. Hot and humid, but at least it was sunny. The year before, the fair had been rained out. Margaret and I did have some help setting up the booth so we were open and ready for business at ten o'clock. By noon the block was filled with people from one end to the other, and Margaret and I had sold a couple of hundred dollars' worth of plants. I was in the middle of selling some lady a hanging geranium when I heard someone calling my name. I turned around and there was Phoebe. She looked terrible. Like she hadn't slept in two weeks. Her eyes were red, and there were big circles under them. Maybe Alex was right. Just add a little torture to the prisoner part.

"What's happened to you?" I said. "I've been calling you all week."

"I know. I'll tell you all about it. Can you get away for a little while?"

"Margaret, do you think I could leave you alone? Phoebe really wants to talk to me about something."

Margaret took one look at Phoebe and waved me away. "Go on. I can handle this by myself."

We pushed our way through the crowds and walked into the park.

"No Dungeon?" I asked.

She shook her head. "I haven't seen him for a week. Mrs. Foster is probably pretty mad, but I couldn't help it."

"What happened to you? Were you really sick?"

"No. Let's go and sit by the fountain above the boat basin, and I'll tell you all about it."

We walked there in silence. I was dying of curiosity and I bet Phoebe knew it. She was just being dramatic.

We settled ourselves down, and after this long silence she started talking.

"My parents told me last week that I'm adopted." She stopped and looked at me.

"You're kidding?"

"Nope. They got me when I was five months old. About Amy's age. And they've kept it a secret all these years. That's what I can't believe. That they never told me."

"Why did they finally tell you?"

"I'd started asking lots of questions. I went through the family photograph albums, and I didn't find anybody who looked like me. I remember when I was about seven years old, some cousin told me I didn't look like anybody in the family. I've been bugged by it ever since, and I used to look through the pictures on my mother's bureau of her parents when they were little. I was trying to see some nose or chin or eye that looked like mine. But there was nothing."

"I don't look like my parents either," I said slowly.

"Yes, you do. Your profile is exactly like your father's. Don't worry. I notice these things. I've always had this feeling of not belonging to Mom and Dad."

I glanced at her face. Her voice sounded sad.

"But they've taken care of you all these years. They love you. Come on, Phoebe, give them a chance. All of us get mad at our parents. Sometimes I feel as if I don't belong to my family, and I'm not adopted."

She didn't say anything for a while. Then, "We had a fight over my marks last week. I didn't do any homework this term. I got into running, and I'm bored with my classes. Dad had a fit because I got a C plus average for the year. He said he was going to make me stop running, and I said I was going to leave home and that they didn't love me anymore." She looked down at her feet. "It went from bad to worse. Finally, I just turned and asked them if they had adopted me. The question really threw them. My mother started to cry, and Dad turned on her and said why did she tell me without discussing it with him first. There they were arguing over telling me and nobody was even looking at me. What a way to find out that your whole life is a lie."

"Why didn't they tell you before?" I asked.

"They said they wanted to protect me from the past, but maybe now it was better that I knew. You know, when I shouted that question at them, I remember I sat there, hoping they would laugh and say what a crazy idea. But the minute I saw my mother's face, I knew I had guessed the big secret." She looked up at me. "It's *not* any better now that I know, Miranda. It's worse. Now I don't really belong to anyone." She started to cry. I put my arm around her shoulder and started patting her clumsily. For a minute, I wished Margaret had been there. She would have given Phoebe one of her bear hugs that squeezes all the sad feelings away.

"We're going to Connecticut tomorrow. Mom says we need to get away together. It's going to be awful. I dread being with them for a whole month up there." She blew her nose and stood up. "I've got to go back. They think I'm going to do something drastic. If I'm out too long, they'll call the police or something."

We walked home slowly. I was trying hard to think of something comforting to say. Phoebe started to talk again.

"When I was a little kid, I used to have this terrible nightmare over and over again. I was sure my mother would leave me somewhere in a crowded place like a store or the circus. I remember one time I had that dream every night for a week. It was horrible."

"Listen, Phoebe, what's your address in Connecticut? We've got to write each other." I pulled out my sales pad and a pen. I wrote down her address and phone number and then mine in Vermont.

"I haven't run for a week," she said as we got to the corner.

"Old mushy muscles," I said with a grin. "You'd better start again or I'll catch up with you. After all, the marathon's in September, and that's just around the corner."

She shrugged. "It seems like years away. Well, bye, Miranda. I'll write you."

"I'll write too." I watched her walk across the street and into her building.

When I got back to the plant booth, there was Mrs. Livingston deep in conversation with Margaret.

"Hello," I said when I walked up.

"Oh, here she is," Margaret said. "Phoebe's mother was wondering where you two had gone."

"Phoebe just went in. We took a walk down to the boat basin."

"That's nice," said Mrs. Livingston. "Well, I'll take the gloxinia and the two big geranium plants. And, you say, the gloxinia will be fine in a northern window?"

"That's the best light for it. And be sure not to water the leaves," Margaret warned. "They turn brown and fall off."

"She seems like a nice woman," Margaret said after Mrs. Livingston had left. "What was wrong with Phoebe? She looked as if she had been crying."

"Her parents just admitted to her that she's adopted. I guess it threw her for a loop."

"That's a tough thing to find out after such a long

time. It's too bad they didn't tell her from the beginning. You'd better move down to the other end of the table, Miranda. I think we've had a couple of the smaller plants stolen."

People were pressing around the table again so we didn't have any more time to talk. It wasn't until later that night that I remembered James, the little boy in the picture.

I went running with Frisbee late that afternoon. It was lonely running without Phoebe, and I ended up talking to Frisbee, which is what I used to do.

"It seems to me, Frisbee, that not everybody is ever happy at the same time as everybody else. One week ago, Phoebe and I were fine and Margaret was sad. Now Margaret feels better and Phoebe feels awful." Frisbee glanced up at me with this bored expression on her face. "What it all boils down to is whether you feel wanted or not. Margaret felt Steven wanted to be with her, and that made her happy. And I felt Margaret didn't want to be with me so that made me sad. Then Steven left Margaret, and she got sad again. And Phoebe feels as if nobody really wants her." People were beginning to look at me strangely so I stopped talking to Frisbee and concentrated on my running.

"I've figured out what my theme in life will be," I said to Alex that night after we turned out the lights. "Never to be left out."

"Why?"

"Because that's what makes most people sad. When they're not wanted. Like Margaret and Steven."

"Not me. I like to be on my own. Who needs all those other people?" He turned over and the bed creaked. Pops had gotten our bunk beds at an army-navy store and they'd never been very sturdy.

When I thought about it, I had to admit that Alex was right about himself. He does like to be on his own. So I decided to stop thinking about life themes and go to sleep. But all night long I kept waking up and thinking about Phoebe lying alone in her room feeling as if she didn't belong to anyone.

I got up early the next morning. Mother was in the kitchen fussing around.

"I know it's Sunday," she said with this guilty expression on her face. "But your father and I decided we'd fix breakfast for you two for a change."

I grinned. "Couldn't take it anymore, Mother? I agree last week was pretty bad. But Alex bought the smelts without asking me if I knew how to cook them. It's part of the low carbohydrate kick he's on."

"Someday that boy will be the death of us all," she said with a sigh. "But he's so earnest about it."

I sat down in a chair and stared out at the river.

"You look tired, Miranda," Mother said. "Is something wrong?"

"Yesterday, Phoebe told me she was adopted. Her

parents just told her. Actually, she guessed and they admitted she was right. She was so sad, Mother. She said she feels as if she doesn't belong to anyone."

Mother stopped fussing in the kitchen and sat down beside me.

"That must be a hard thing to hear when you're thirteen years old. It's too bad they didn't tell her right from the beginning. It would have seemed more natural, not such a secret." We sat in silence for a moment.

"I wasn't very good at cheering her up," I said slowly. "I couldn't think of the right thing to say."

"I'm sure the Livingstons love her very much. After all, they chose to adopt her. That should make her feel pretty special. A lot of women have babies that they don't want."

I thought about that for a while. "Did you want me and Alex?" I asked.

Mother smiled. "I knew that would be the next question. Of course we did. But we were lucky to be able to have it that way."

"Where's breakfast?" Pops asked. "You two seem to be sitting down on the job here."

"Why don't you call her up, Miranda? See how she's feeling," asked Mother.

"She's already left for Connecticut. I might write her a letter though. I've got her address," I said

"That's a good idea," said Mother. "It would be

even more special if you wrote her a letter."

So that afternoon I wrote Phoebe a letter saying I thought I knew how she felt, and I was sure her parents loved her very much because, after all, they'd chosen to have her, and I missed her already. I mailed it when I went running that afternoon.

# 11 · We Go to Vermont

The first day we got up to Vermont I spent my time with Grandpa. He took me around and showed me how the animals were and which field he was haying and how much weeding the vegetable garden needed. The grand tour we call it.

Even though I like living in New York, I could get used to the country too. Except in the winter. All that cold weather and the feeling of being closed in for so many months would drive me buggy.

"Where's the pony?" I asked as we stood at the edge of the pasture.

"She died last winter," Grandpa said. "I thought I wrote you about it. She got out of the pasture and headed off into the woods. We found her a week later, frozen stiff."

"How sad," I said.

"Sensible animal," said Grandpa. "She knew her time had come. Maybe she wanted to be alone. Let's go down to the garden. I want to show you the new section."

I walked along beside him, glancing up at his face now and then. Grandpa is very handsome. He has this thin face and bright blue eyes. Mother says he used to have curly hair like hers but now it's straight and completely white.

"I've fenced this part off because I want to experiment with the vegetables in here. See if they grow any better."

"They look about the same to me."

He laughed. "I think you're right. And you wouldn't believe how much work I did on this part. I dug down eighteen inches for every row and put in fertilizer so the roots would hit there first. It's a new French method."

My grandfather used to work on Wall Street in a big bank. Then suddenly he quit and moved to Vermont. My mother said everyone was horrified except my grandmother, who must have known how unhappy he'd been all along. Grandpa likes to think of himself as a simple country farmer, but when you get him talking he's just as well read as the next person.

I whistled for Frisbee, who had slipped through

the gate with us. She was madly digging up something in one corner.

"Yes, you stay out of there, Frisbee," Grandfather said. "The pond's the next stop. I've built up the dam so you can't touch bottom in the middle anymore."

"You've been working hard, Grandpa," I said with a smile.

He put his arm around my shoulders. "You know me, Miranda. I don't want to slow down. One day I'll drop in my tracks while I'm milking the cows or haying the fields. It's the only way to go."

I didn't say anything because I don't like to think about him ever dying.

"Your mother says Margaret is a special friend of yours," he said.

"I've told you about her before. She's the one who lives in our building. She loves the city, and we do a lot of exploring together. The zoo and museums and movies. She's been all over the world and she's read thousands of books. I know you'll like her."

"I'm sure I'll like her. But she'll probably be bored by an old country bumpkin like me."

"You're the only country bumpkin I know who's trying out the French method of gardening," I said with a snort.

He just shrugged and kept on walking. Grandpa doesn't fool me.

After looking things over, Margaret decided that she'd be better off in the cottage by herself.

"I hope you don't mind, Miranda. I'd love to share your room, but I have some very peculiar habits. Sometimes I like to read late at night or get up early in the morning and do my exercises. Who knows? I may even snore," she added with a laugh.

"That's all right," I said. "Alex and I are used to each other." I saw him rolling his eyes but for once he kept his big mouth shut. Actually, deep down inside, I was just as happy. I like Margaret very much, but I don't think I would have felt comfortable sharing a room with her for two whole weeks.

We settled in very easily together. I went running with Frisbee every morning and puttered around with Grandpa and read my reading list for school, which as usual I had left till the end of the summer. Grandpa discovered Margaret liked to fish (she is always surprising me), so they went off every afternoon to this secret stream that Grandpa discovered last summer. Grandpa was delighted. We were all bored by fishing and he hadn't really had a fishing companion since my grandmother died. My father set up his easel in the barn in an old tack room that Grandpa didn't use anymore.

Mother took long walks with Margaret to pick wild flowers and she and I went swimming in the mud hole and did the shopping and she baked huge blue-

berry pies, which she never has time to do at home.
Alex spent most of the time driving Grandpa's car
around on the dirt roads because he was practicing
for his license, which he can't even get in New York
for two more years. Typical.

I got a letter from Phoebe at the end of the first
week we were there. It was very odd.

*Dear Miranda,*

*Thanks for your letter. Sometimes I wish Mom and
Dad had chosen someone else. Things aren't going
very well here. The only time I can think is when I
go out running but yesterday I couldn't even get up
to three miles. Maybe you'll have to go into that
marathon without me. But who knows where I'll be
or what I'll be doing by then. I'm considering several
drastic alternatives. Will keep you posted.*

*Until soon,*

*Phoebe*

Little did I know that she had already taken one of
the drastic alternatives.

It must have been that first weekend that her parents called. Mrs. Livingston sounded panicked. She
got Mother on the phone first. I was sitting in the
kitchen snapping the ends off the green beans, so I

could hear my mother's end of the conversation. It went something like this.

"Oh, yes, of course, how are you?"

Silence.

"Oh, no. That doesn't sound like her at all."

Silence. I was really pricking up my ears. Mother kept glancing at me with this strange look on her face.

"No. She hasn't been here. She wouldn't come this far, would she?" Silence.

"Aren't there some relatives she might go to?"

Short silence.

"Yes, of course, you would have thought of that."

By that time I had figured it out. Phoebe had run away.

"Yes, she's right here. I'll put her on."

My mother covered up the phone with the palm of her hand.

"It's Phoebe's mother," she whispered. "Phoebe disappeared yesterday, and they are very worried about her. She wants to talk to you."

I got up to take the phone, but my mother held it for another minute.

"Miranda, I saw you got a letter from Phoebe the other day. You must tell her mother everything you know, even if it means being disloyal to your friend. Phoebe is too young to be wandering around alone."

I nodded and picked up the phone. "Hello?"

"Miranda, this is Mrs. Livingston. Do you have any idea where Phoebe might have gone?"

"No, I don't. I'm sorry."

"Did she say anything to you before you left?"

"No," I said slowly, trying to think back. "I got a letter from her this week that was sort of strange. She said things weren't going very well and that I may have to go into the marathon without her."

Mrs. Livingston was silent for a minute. "She didn't say anything else?"

"No," I lied. There didn't seem to be any point to mentioning the line about the drastic alternatives. That would just make her think Phoebe had gone off and killed herself or something.

"Miranda, I'm going to have to notify the police if she doesn't turn up soon. You know our number here. I want you to call me immediately if you hear anything from her. All right?"

"Yes, I will," I said. She said good-bye and hung up.

I sat down at the table and went back to snapping the beans. My mother's eyes on me made me uncomfortable even though I had nothing to hide.

"Phoebe was dreading this month with her parents," I said thoughtfully. "It must have gotten really bad."

"Do you know where she'd go, Miranda? You realize how serious this is."

"Yes, Mother. No, I don't have any idea where

she'd go." I finished the beans as quickly as I could and went looking for Alex.

He didn't seem very surprised by the news about Phoebe, which made me think that he knew something. Ever since they'd gone off to buy my shoes together, they'd been quite friendly.

"No, I didn't know her plans. Phoebe's smart. She can be private when she wants to. But I know her parents have been driving her crazy. And then on top of that, to find out that the parents who have been driving you crazy aren't really your parents. It must make you sit and dream about your real parents and wonder if they'd have been any better."

"I know," I said. "You could spend all your time dreaming up all sorts of wonderful parents who were rich and never punished you and let you eat whatever you wanted and lived in a mansion."

"That sounds like Phoebe's parents," Alex said dryly as he went out of the room.

# 12 · The Drastic Alternative

I sat around the next day waiting for some news but nobody called. I kept racking my brains, trying to think about where Phoebe might go. The only inspiration I had was that she could be hiding out in the Fosters' apartment. But then I decided Mrs. Foster wouldn't put up with that. Just a couple of weeks ago, she had asked Phoebe to stop dropping in all the time.

Mother kept watching me as if she wasn't sure I'd told her the whole truth. But after a while, when I didn't slip off to a clandestine meeting by the mailbox, I guess she gave up. By the time we sat down to dinner, I was really getting worried. And mad at Phoebe for making me worried. I hoped she had enough sense not to talk to any strange men at bus stops or accept rides in cars.

"No word about Phoebe?" Margaret asked. I shook my head.

"You look wonderful," I said suddenly because I'd just noticed how tan her face was. She had two red spots high on her cheekbones. She laughed at me.

"It's the country air and your grandfather's jokes," she said. "He's not the quietest fisherman I've ever known."

"Now, Margaret, you do your share of talking too," he said quickly. They smiled at each other and there was a tiny moment of silence around the table. My, my, I thought to myself. What do we have here? When I suggested that Margaret come up to Vermont, I'd never put her together in my mind with my grandfather. The vision of Steven was still too strong, and I'd just thought she would recuperate quietly. That shows you how little I know.

It was Alex's turn to do the dishes, so I went up to the room right after dinner. First I tried to go to sleep, but I was much too restless. I was sitting there wondering if it was too dark to go running when I heard somebody calling me from outside. I thought it was Margaret on her way across the lawn to the cottage, but when I leaned out and answered there was nobody there. Now I'm really cracking up, I said to myself. But about two minutes later, someone called again and this time I jumped to the window. There she was, Phoebe Livingston, alive and well, standing in the bushes by the porch.

"Phoebe," I yelled. "What are you doing here?"

"Never mind that," she said. "Keep your voice down. Is anybody in your room?"

"Not yet. Alex is still doing the dishes."

"Can I get up there without anybody seeing me?"

Just then, the screen door on the front porch slammed. Phoebe dove back into the bushes. Margaret and Grandpa came down the porch steps and stood looking up at the sky.

"It's beautiful, tonight, isn't it?" Margaret said. "Funny how in New York you can forget to look at the sky for days on end."

"That's another reason not to live there," Grandpa said with a snort.

I was going nuts sitting up above, listening to them. Also I felt strange since I knew they didn't know I was there.

"Good night, Margaret. Good night, Grandpa," I called.

They turned around quickly. "Have you seen the stars, Miranda?" Margaret called. "The sky is so clear tonight."

"Yes," I said, glancing down at Phoebe. She was crouched by the porch about ten feet away from them.

"See you in the morning, Miranda," Grandpa said, and he took Margaret's arm to walk her to the cottage.

We waited until they were quite far away before we said anything. "Those two look like a couple of lovebirds," Phoebe said with a giggle.

"What are you going to do?" I asked.

"How can I get up there?"

"If you did it now, you could come right up the front stairs. I can still hear the others talking in the kitchen. I'll come down and meet you on the porch. We've got to hurry because Grandpa will be back any minute."

We got upstairs without anybody seeing us, but just as she settled down on the bed, we heard Alex coming along the hall.

"Quick, in the closet." I threw her bags under the bed and was sitting down again when he sauntered in.

"What's up?" he said, glancing at my face.

"Nothing. Why?" I was trying to sound as casual as possible, but I have to admit, I'm the worst liar in the world.

"You look very guilty," he said, sitting down on his bed across the room. "And from this position, I can see somebody's suitcase under your bed." He smiled. "All right, Phoebe, come on out of the closet."

Maybe Alex should be a detective. Even Sherlock Holmes couldn't have figured it out that fast. But the clues were pretty obvious, and I guess I couldn't have kept Phoebe in the closet all night. The door creaked

open slowly and she stepped out, looking a little foolish.

"Hi, Alex," she said quietly. Then she sat down on
my bed and started to cry. Alex and I looked at each
other in despair.

"Come on, Phoebe," I said putting my arm around
her. "It can't be that bad. We'll call your parents and
they can come up and get you."

She drew away. "No, that's the last thing I want.
I'm not ever going back to them." She stopped crying and blew her nose with a crumpled old Kleenex.

"Hey, Phoebe, how did you get here?" Alex asked.
"Did you run up?" He was looking down at her feet.
She had on her running shoes.

That made her laugh, which certainly made me
feel better because I never know what to do when
somebody cries.

"I took the bus part of the way, and then I hitchhiked the rest."

I gasped. "You hitchhiked? Haven't you read all
the terrible stories about accepting rides from stran-
gers?"

"No. But the old couple who gave me the ride from
town told them to me. They wanted to drive me
right up to the front door, but I convinced them that
I was surprising your grandfather for his birthday."

"You certainly will be a surprise," Alex said
thoughtfully.

"You can't tell them," Phoebe said. "I'm going right now if you tell them."

She stood up and started pulling her bags out from under the bed. "Don't worry," I said, pulling her arm. "We're not going to tell anyone."

She sat down again with a bump. "Do you think you could get some food for me?" she asked. "I haven't eaten anything since breakfast this morning."

"I'll get you something," Alex said. I was glad that he left because it gave me a chance to ask Phoebe some questions.

"What's been happening?" I asked.

"Well, the first couple of days they wanted to talk to me all the time. But whenever I tried to ask about who I really am or where I'm from or why they never told me before, Mother would say that was my past and we must look to the future. Then they gave up talking to me completely. Dad plays golf with his friends all day and Mom busies herself around the house. Finally I couldn't stand it anymore. I started having those dreams about being left places again. So I left."

"They're worried about you. Your mother called us yesterday and said I had to call her if you came here."

"You won't do that, will you, Miranda? Please?" She was looking at me with this kind of desperate look in her face.

"Well, I'm not going to do anything tonight." We were both silent for a minute. "You could stay up here with us for the next week. I mean, I bet if Mother called your parents and invited you, they would let you stay."

"Oh, no, after this, they're never going to let me out of their sight again. Dad will probably hire a bodyguard for me."

"But, Phoebe, what are you going to do? You can't just wander around the world for the rest of your life." I was beginning to feel very depressed. How could I let Phoebe go off somewhere without telling anybody? And if I told on her, she'd never forgive me.

Alex came in with a plate of food. After she'd finished it, she lay down on my bed. I got my old sleeping bag out of the closet and rolled it out between the beds. Alex turned off the light, and we lay there for a while without saying anything.

Finally Phoebe spoke, and her voice had this eerie sound in the dark room. I felt as if she were talking to us from a million miles away.

"When you find out you're adopted it's like having your whole world turned upside down. I don't have any roots anymore. Dad's father isn't really my grandfather. And what about all the talents and diseases that are supposed to be passed along to you in your blood? Who knows? My father may have been a marathon runner."

Alex didn't say anything and neither did I. I lay still waiting for her to go to sleep.

"Phoebe?" There was no answer.

Alex sat up. "She's asleep," he whispered, looking over at the other bed. "What are you going to do?"

"Me?" I said. My voice sounded squeaky. "We're in this together, brother dear. You know she's here too."

"All right, calm down. What did she tell you while I was downstairs?" Alex asked.

So I told him what Phoebe had said.

"I see what she means," he said quietly. "It must make you feel very lost. But she can't just run away. She's got to try and talk to her parents about it."

"For once, Dr. Bartlett, I agree with you."

We decided to try and convince Phoebe of that in the morning.

But she would have none of it. "I *have* tried to talk to them. They are impossible. They just want our lives to run along smoothly the way they did before. Don't ask any questions, Phoebe. Just be our good little adopted daughter."

The three of us sat looking at each other, and nobody knew what to say next. We finally decided that Alex and I should go downstairs and have breakfast so that nobody would get suspicious. Then we'd bring some food up to Phoebe and discuss where to go from there.

There were about fifty times during that meal that

I opened my mouth to say something. Mother wondered out loud whether anybody had heard from Phoebe, and Grandpa said how terrible it must be for the Livingstons not knowing where she was. I felt Alex's eyes on me the whole time but I didn't dare look at him. Well, it turned out the whole charade was for nothing because by the time we got back upstairs, she was gone. There was a note on my bed.

*Dear Miranda and Alex,*

*I'm going now. Thank you for putting me up for the night. I know that you don't really understand what I'm going through. Eventually you would feel bound to tell your parents. I'm scared about going off alone but I have to get away. Maybe I will come back soon. But I have to think about everything all by myself for a while.*

*Love,*

*Phoebe*

This time I was really scared for her. Where was she going to go next?

"She's got a lot of money," Alex explained slowly. "She'll be all right for a while."

"I'm going to tell Mother," I said, heading for the door.

Alex jumped up to stop me. "Give her a day," he said. "Maybe that's all she needs. Anyway, the police are going to find her soon. If you tell now, they'll pick her up right away, and then she'll be furious with us too."

I looked at him. I knew he was right. What could happen to her in one day? And she'd never speak to us again if she thought we'd told on her. I sat back down on the bed with all these thoughts whirling through my head. Just then we heard a car coming down the main driveway. Alex looked out. I heard the car door slam and then Grandpa's footsteps on the front porch.

"Who is it?" I asked Alex.

"The Martins. That old couple who run the drugstore." He pushed the window open and leaned out to listen.

When he pulled his head back in, his face was white. "Brace yourself, old girl. The jig's up."

"What are you talking about?"

"That's the old couple who picked Phoebe up at the bus station yesterday. They just saw her heading out the other side of town so they decided to come investigate."

"Miranda," Mother called from the bottom of the stairs. My heart dropped. Alex looked at me.

"You're in this too," I muttered. Together we went slowly downstairs.

"Was Phoebe here last night?" Mother asked.

I didn't say anything.

"Miranda." I'd never heard that tone in her voice and it scared me.

"Yes. She left this morning when we were down at breakfast. Alex and I were going to try and keep her here and convince her to call her parents but she ran away before we got back."

"Why didn't you tell us last night?" Mother asked.

"Never mind about that," my father said. "Let's go find her."

Things happened fast after that. My parents found Phoebe hitchhiking on the little road that goes north out of town. When they slowed down to pick her up, she recognized them and started to run. Pops caught her easily. You should have seen the look she gave us when they brought her in the house.

"We didn't tell," Alex said quickly. "They found out from the old couple who gave you a ride yesterday." Alex is always trying to save his skin. I didn't say anything.

"Face it, Phoebe," my father said. "You wouldn't have gotten very far anyway."

"I got all the way up here," she said triumphantly. Her eyes looked all shiny and I knew she didn't want to cry in front of everybody but it was getting hard to hold back the tears. Just then, Margaret came in. She took one look at Phoebe and went up and hugged her. Well, that did Phoebe in. She broke down and cried on Margaret's shoulder. We all shifted around uncomfortably, and my mother blew her nose.

My father went and called the Livingstons. He told them about a nearby airport they could fly to where he could go pick them up. Phoebe wouldn't talk to me all day while we were waiting for her parents. When I heard the car in the driveway, I went up to my bedroom. I didn't want to see the scene between all of them.

Alex came up after a while. I was lying on my bed, staring at the ceiling.

"She's staying with us," he said.

"What?" I asked.

"Margaret talked them into it. Phoebe's going to share the cottage with her, and Margaret's taking full responsibility that she doesn't run away again. Margaret thinks Phoebe needs a chance to think about everything. She and her parents aren't really ready to talk to each other." He shook his head. "That Margaret is really something."

"How is she going to keep Phoebe here?" I said. "She'll run away as soon as she gets a chance."

But she didn't. That first night, I sat by the window and looked across the lawn toward the cottage. The lights were still on down there when I finally went to bed at eleven o'clock.

Phoebe wouldn't talk to me. She stuck by Margaret like glue. They took long walks and went swimming down in the mud hole.

"Don't be hurt, Miranda," Mother said to me. But I was, and she knew it. "You know what a good listener Margaret is. Phoebe's finally found somebody who will listen to her all day long. And Phoebe's got a lot stored up inside of her."

"I miss them both," I said. "Plus I'm jealous," I admitted.

"Isn't it nice to have two of your friends like each other? After all, you're the reason they came together. Without you, Phoebe might be stuck back in Connecticut with her parents or running away again."

I hadn't thought about it that way before. It did make me feel better.

I went back to my running. I was up to four and a half miles, but I didn't seem to be getting any better. I'd decided not to go into the marathon after all. It would be terrible not to finish.

I ran in the early mornings before breakfast. It's the best time of day in Vermont. Everything's completely still except the birds and the big red sun coming up over the fields. The whole world seems to belong to me.

One morning just as I passed the mailbox, Phoebe came out from behind the cottage and fell into step with me. I didn't say anything. I wasn't sure how happy I was to have her with me. We ran for a long time in silence. Just the *plop-plop* of our feet on the dirt road, the noisy morning birds, and our rhythmic breathing. I decided I wasn't going to be the first one to slow down, no matter how much it hurt. So we ran and we ran and we ran. It was like some strange endless contest. My legs felt like lead and my whole chest ached. Finally she gave in.

"You win," she screamed, pulling on my arm. We both collapsed gasping by the side of the road. It took us at least ten minutes just to breathe normally again. I got my inhaler out and sprayed it into my mouth. The taste of the medicine always makes me gag. I shuddered as I sucked it in, but the wheezing was already better.

"No attacks, please," Phoebe said. "I couldn't possibly go for help."

I smiled and shook my head.

"How many miles do you think we ran?" she asked.

"At least five. I've been running four and a half and we went farther than that this time."

"Oh, I think it's about six. One marathon at least."

"Are you still going into the marathon?" I asked.

"Of course. Aren't you?"

I shrugged. "I'm not sure. It would be horrible to go in and not finish."

"There you go again," she said with a smile. "I

can't run because I have asthma. Translation by Phoebe Livingston. I don't want to try because I might fail."

"Shut up," I said but there wasn't much conviction in my voice.

We started to walk home slowly. We must have gone the first mile in complete silence. I was beginning to feel mad that we'd run so far because it meant we had to walk that whole way back together. Finally she said something.

"I know you didn't tell until they'd already found out," she said. "Margaret told me."

"Why are you acting so mad at me then?" I burst out. "You won't even look at me at dinner."

"But you wouldn't look at me either. And you never come down to the cottage to see me and Margaret. You've been acting as if you wished I'd go home."

I couldn't think of a thing to say. We'd wasted all this time being mad at each other when we could have been doing things together.

"I didn't think you wanted me near you. You and Margaret seemed so caught up with each other."

Phoebe nodded. "She is the most amazing lady."

"Didn't I tell you that ages ago?" I said. I was happy she could understand why Margaret meant so much to me.

"Do you know that she adopted a little boy?"

"Yes."

"He died when he was five years old. Isn't that sad? He had some hereditary disease which they didn't know about until it was too late." She stopped walking for a minute. "Margaret thinks they should let people at least see the records of the natural parents for health problems if nothing else."

I didn't say anything.

"Margaret's good to talk to because she can see what I'm saying about not knowing my roots and all, but she can also see Mom and Dad's point of view. I didn't think about how I was hurting them. Always before, I kept thinking about my side of things, and I shouted at them a lot. Now I'd like to go back and try to talk to them." She glanced at me. "What do you think, Miranda?"

"I wasn't saying anything because I always seem to say the wrong thing when we're talking about your adoption. You keep telling me I don't understand."

She grabbed my arm to stop me. "I didn't mean that, Miranda," she said softly. "I think I've been saying a lot of things I didn't mean."

I just nodded and kept walking, but I had this lump in my throat. When I looked at her that one moment, I thought, "This is really my best friend. I finally have a best friend, and it's going to stay that way forever."

# 13 · Marathon Miranda

It turned out we got to stay in Vermont a whole extra week. When Mother and Pops had to go back to New York, Margaret offered to stay with us kids and bring us home on the bus. Of course, Grandpa liked that idea because it meant he got to see more of Margaret. The Livingstons were reluctant at first, but when they heard Phoebe talking they could tell that things were much better.

We ran every morning. Alex went back in the car and measured the distance we'd run. It turned out to be a little over six miles. That gave me hope because it meant I could go that distance if I wanted to.

During the extra week, I showed Phoebe the farm. We helped Grandpa do a lot of the chores because he kept getting distracted by Margaret. I showed

Phoebe the secret places in the basement of the barn where they used to keep the horses and the way the stream fell into a waterfall down behind the chicken coop. One night we drove into town for a bingo game, and I won five dollars which made Alex furious because he was just one number behind me. It was a wonderful week, and I felt terrible when Grandpa drove us into town to the bus station.

Everybody was feeling sad. We kissed and hugged Grandpa and the three of us got on the bus. I peeked out the window and watched Margaret giving him this big hug. Just like Margaret.

"Don't spy on them," Alex said to me. "It's not fair."

"Do you think they'll get married?" Phoebe asked.

"I hope so," I said quickly. "Wouldn't it be wonderful? Except that I'd hate to have Margaret move away from New York."

When she got on the bus, we all looked at her expectantly but she just sat down across the aisle and got out her book of crossword puzzles.

"Not even a tear," Alex whispered to me.

"Maybe it means she knows she's coming back," I whispered.

"I don't want to go home," Phoebe wailed as the bus pulled on to the highway. "Times like these should go on forever."

"Then they'd get boring," Alex said. Always the practical one.

"Why don't you read your magazine, Alex?" I said. He was driving me crazy hanging over us that way.

"I get the hint," he muttered and subsided into his seat.

"Are you nervous about seeing your parents?" I asked.

Phoebe nodded. "All these great ideas I've had up here may just fall apart when I see Mom and Dad." She glanced at me. "I had a strange dream last night. I dreamt that I found my real mother. She was tall and had short dark hair and she looked just like me. I went running up to her and she turned away. I kept trying to make her turn around so I could see her face again but she wouldn't. She disappeared into thin air like a ghost."

I shivered. "What a sad dream," I said softly.

Phoebe didn't answer. She was looking out the window, and I couldn't see her face.

When we got home, Margaret went up with Phoebe to the Livingstons. I could tell Phoebe was scared to see them again. I was dying to call her that night but Mother convinced me not to.

"Let her figure out how she feels about everything before she has to tell you."

"Mother, do you think Margaret will marry Grandpa?" I asked at dinner.

"Did he ask her?" Mother said.

"I don't know," I admitted. "But they seemed to be very close."

"It would be nice for Grandpa to have the company. Especially Margaret, who is so smart and relaxed and good-humored. But I think she might go nuts up there on the farm. She's always lived in the city."

"This is all jumping the gun a bit," Pops said. "Let the poor man propose before you marry them off."

Phoebe and I met in the park at the usual time the next day.

"Let's run first," she said. "Then I'll tell you everything."

It was hard to get back to running in the heat and the pollution after the clear, cool Vermont air. I was gasping for breath after two miles.

"Go on," I waved to Phoebe when I slowed down to a walk. "I can't keep it up."

When she circled back, she found me collapsed on a park bench.

"This is terrible," I said. "Take me back to Vermont before I die."

She nodded and sat down. "At least, we have a week to practice before the marathon."

I didn't answer. I still hadn't decided whether to run in the marathon or not.

"No second thoughts," she said to me. "I entered you this morning."

My face fell. "You're going to do just fine," she said. "You've been training more than I have."

"But you don't have these pathetic lungs," I said in a pleading voice.

She shook her head firmly. Just then, Frisbee came up and licked her legs. That habit of Frisbee's drives me nuts. She likes the salty taste of sweat.

"Dungeon and the Fosters are still away," Phoebe said, patting Frisbee.

"How was last night?"

"Better than I thought it would be. Margaret was right. We just needed a little vacation from each other. Mom and I had a long talk alone. I told her I wished they cared more about my running, and I wanted Dad to stop calling me 'Goose.' All the things I've been trying to tell them all along, but this time I think she heard me. I was so glad Margaret came up to the apartment because it helped to break the ice." Phoebe smiled. "Thanks again for having me in Vermont."

"Well, I didn't invite you," I said, drawing myself up haughtily. "You crashed."

She burst out laughing and we decided to walk to Broadway together.

The weather on the day of the marathon was beautiful. It was one of those brisk, windy September days with big white clouds in the sky.

"Just like Vermont," Phoebe said. We were all walking over together. Mother took a day off from work when I told her we were really going to run it. Pops and Alex and the Livingstons came too and, just as we were going down into the park, I heard someone shouting and there was Margaret, running across the street against the light. "Late as usual," I whispered to Phoebe and she laughed.

After that, it happened really fast. They gave us numbers (I was 579) and lined us up. Everybody was standing around warming up, touching their toes and stretching their legs. As I was standing there looking through my legs at Central Park upside down, I had a little laugh when I thought of all the times I'd sneered at the people doing this in Riverside Park. And here I was just as crazy as the rest of them.

Phoebe squeezed my hand and whispered good luck, and the gun went off and we started to run. It was pretty crowded at first, but after a while some people dropped out and the rest of us spread out along the track. Phoebe disappeared up ahead of me, and I tried not to think about anything except keeping it all even. The only way I was going to make it was if I didn't panic. One, two, buckle my shoe, three, four. It must have been at about the second mile that I swung into the rhythm, and I knew I was all right. As long as I kept the rhythm, I knew I could run forever.

Phoebe was there at the finish line with Mother and Pops and Alex and Margaret. They were all cheering and screaming, which was a little foolish since I was about number 1,379, but it did make me feel good. Then they hugged me and kissed me (except for Alex) even though I was all sweaty. I have to admit I felt terrific.

"How did you do?" I yelled at Phoebe.

"Forty-fifth."

"Fantastic," I screamed and hugged her again.

Just then, Alex came up and hung this big card around my neck that said MARATHON MIRANDA. Well, I just about died laughing, and in the end I hugged him too, which made him blush and push me away. Then we all went off to Baskin-Robbins to celebrate.